T0365927

e-THERAPY

e-THERAPY

Where Shadows Meet

RICHARD CARR

ARCHWAY
PUBLISHING

Archway Publishing books may be ordered through booksellers or by contacting:

Archway Publishing
1663 Liberty Drive
Bloomington, IN 47403
www.archwaypublishing.com
844-669-3957

ISBN: 978-1-6657-6946-4 (sc)
ISBN: 978-1-6657-6947-1 (e)

Library of Congress Control Number: 2024927253

Print information available on the last page.

Archway Publishing rev. date: 01/23/2025

Chapter One

ILEEN DUET WAS ABOUT TO MAKE THE WORST MISTAKE OF HER life. This was not one of those mistakes that build character, when you ruffle a child's hair, pat her on the back and say—with an exaggerated wink—*you're learning*. No, it was nothing like that. And besides, Eileen was no innocent child. Rather, it was one of those decisions that can ruin a person's life. There would be no learning from this mistake, which was rather unusual because Eileen was paid to solve other people's problems. She was a therapist, and even if her judgment was particularly keen when it came to the problems of her patients, she wasn't quite able—as many of us aren't—to take advantage of this useful skill for her own good.

One summer evening, as nightfall was coming sooner and the air was turning cooler, Eileen sat alone in the kitchen, pushing around the remains of a lukewarm, too salty microwave dinner. She finished, dumped it into the garbage and walked into the living room where she paused for a moment to enjoy the sound of rain pelting against the window. It was a heavy, steady downpour that felt comforting in an otherwise silent and dark house. Somehow it took her mind away from how alone she was in her marriage. Bright sun and nice weather seemed only to remind her of how others might be taking advantage of a beautiful day.

Spotting the light escaping underneath the basement door she called to her husband, Ron. There was no answer. "Ron? You down there?"

"What?" he called back.

"I'll be in the study. I've got some work to catch up on. You need anything?" she asked.

"No. What is it you want?"

"I didn't want anything. I was asking if you...." She winced, then finished, "I was just asking if you needed something."

She waited, but he didn't answer.

"Do you need anything?" she called again.

"I'm watching something. Will you just let me be. For God sakes, can't I just have some time alone?" he pleaded. Eileen squeezed her fists tightly a couple of times, then ran her hand through her hair and took a deep breath. Her lips pressed tightly together. She thought about responding, fidgeted for awhile, but then said nothing.

Giving up with a sigh of disgust, she walked into the study and turned on the computer. She leaned back and listened to the whirring and whizzing as it booted up.

The Duets were married, but living quite alone after 10 years. They usually didn't yell at each other; rather, like many couples their marriage was characterized by annoyance, intolerance, aggravation, and irritation. They had drifted apart and now seemed to accelerate on their separate ways. The computer offered an escape and some pleasure to Eileen, whereas the T.V., newspapers and long work hours occupied Ron's time.

As a way of coping with her sorry marriage, Eileen was fast learning the ways of the Internet. It was 1996, and the online world was still a novelty, a Wild West of dial-up connections and chat rooms. She enjoyed its immense size and her connection to seemingly millions of others just like her. She craved the closeness and intimacy that was found among the anonymous strangers in a virtual world that was then dubbed "Cyberspace" as a nod to its uncharted vastness. Ron, on the other hand, was content with a peaceful coexistence. He didn't need to *cope;* he just wanted her to leave him alone. So here they were—Ron down the basement, Eileen in the study.

Eileen was in her forties, petite and attractive with an athletic build. She kept her shoulder-length auburn hair pulled back in a pony tail. Her thin lips, outlined a broad smile she flashed often. People were drawn to her, and so becoming a therapist seemed inevitable. She was warm and sincere, but most of all she was skillful at deflecting questions about herself, usually turning a conversation onto you. She listened intently, and sometime later, when you ran into her at the supermarket or saw her on one of her long nightly walks she would ask, "How is your brother-in-law doing? Did he have the operation?" or, "How does your sister like her new job?" She remembered everything about you, and people liked that. Nothing was too mundane or trivial for her. She made you feel good about yourself.

Eileen's younger sister, Kelly, was grateful for the two years Eileen spent running back and forth to care for Kelly's twin daughters while Kelly's husband was dying of cancer. On Thursdays, when Eileen worked evenings at a community mental health center affiliated with Milltown Valley Hospital, she'd spend her mornings driving across two towns to help her sister get the kids off to school. On Mondays and Wednesdays, when her workday ended at five o'clock, she'd go directly to Kelly's house to help with dinner, baths, and bedtime.

On many days, Kelly returned home well after ten o'clock at night (and sometimes close to midnight). She seemed as unable to manage her time as she was inadequate at caring for her children, though Eileen attributed this to stress, not to some character flaw. She figured Kelly coped with her husband's tragedy by losing herself in work (she was a paralegal) or in shopping. Everyone deals with loss differently, Eileen believed, and whatever Kelly was doing to keep herself sane should be respected.

Eileen was the rescuer in her family. As children, it was Eileen who comforted her sister when their father came home drunk. He came home drunk often, and often he was dangerous. The solution to this was simple in Eileen's eyes: stay out of his way, don't argue or disagree with him, and put a smile on your face. "Everything's okay, daddy. You okay? Can I get you something?" she'd ask. And it was always, "Yeah, you can get your fuckin' mother out of my life. Can ya do that for me? Can you?" Eileen would strain a smile and tremble. Just keep the peace, she'd think. Just keep the peace.

Her father was a tall, burly man, balding but with a smattering of dark unkempt hair around the sides and back of his head; a ruddy complexion, slightly bowed legs, and thick hands. He always seemed to be sweating. And he always seemed to be angry at someone or about something. He was, quite simply, as close to a monster as a man can be.

He sometimes disappeared for days, but eventually would return with a new complaint about his wife or children. "I'm sick and tired of this shit in my way when I come home. This is going to change!" he'd bellow. Or he'd clench his teeth and with his alcohol reddened eyes looking as though they were aflame, he'd roar at his wife in the most dramatic and menacing tone, "Do you see where you left my mail? Do you? This is gonna stop. This shit's really gonna stop! I told you exactly how and where I want my mail left!" Then he'd lean closer and closer, straining his neck until he was nose to nose with his wife, whose only response was to recoil in fear (or to avoid suffocating on his stinking breath).

His pattern of disappearing and reappearing with a vengeance kept the family on edge even in his absence. And so, social work seemed a perfect fit for Eileen. It is unimaginable how she managed to complete homework, but she somehow disconnected from the shouting around her to become a straight "A" student through school—a perfectionist. Socially, she avoided having friends over in order to keep her family secret, but she was popular nonetheless. Focusing on other people's problems, being a good listener, and avoiding conflicts were useful skills not only for winning friends, but also for staying in the good graces of her volatile father; the downside was you just never get to know yourself.

Eileen met her husband many years ago. They were high school sweethearts who ended their relationship during senior year of college. Ron became a financial analyst afterwards, and Eileen pursued a social work degree. They ran into each other one day about eleven years ago at the grocery store, where Eileen had stopped on one of her back and forth treks to her sister's house. Six months later they were married.

They first lived just outside Philadelphia, before moving to New Jersey when Ron's career landed him in Manhattan. Milltown, New Jersey was a medium-sized, nondescript town burrowed among the many small suburban communities just west of New York City. Ron worked long hours and commuted into the city, whereas Eileen's commute was all of three minutes to the local community mental health center right in Milltown.

Instead of working in the study, a lie she was more regularly telling her husband, this evening Eileen was logged onto her computer to play. She had long overcome the guilt associated with what seemed initially like a monumental waste of time. Her only concern now was that she would be playing online while her husband was home and still awake. *There really isn't anything wrong with entertaining myself, is there?* she'd try to convince herself. After all, millions of people were doing it. Nevertheless, she'd quickly exit the screen or shut the computer down if she heard her husband coming upstairs or walking by the study. She found it difficult to assert her right to do what she found enjoyable, even when *he* was free to do as he pleased. She'd feel silly or stupid, she thought, if her husband discovered she was spending this much time on the

Internet—it was a risk, however, she was willing to take for the closeness she yearned for and wasn't getting from him.

Eileen was still a novice with the computer when a friend at work introduced her to the world of online chatting. Initially, she used the computer—which Ron had bought her as a birthday present less than a year ago—to track their bills, to organize paperwork for her private patients, and to browse the Internet. In time, however, she was exclusively logging on to chat—using the nickname *Cheeryl*—to a variety of people she met from all over the world. Some of the chat was boring, and some men were downright perverts. But most people, she learned, were fascinating, whether they were doctors, lawyers, truck drivers, homemakers, or college students. Everyone seemed to have a story to tell. Tonight Cheeryl met Sweetdude35.

Eileen didn't chat much. That is, she didn't offer much input, but she watched a lot. She mostly read other people's quips, comments, and what often seemed like inside banter strewn with a variety of initials—a clue to a person's online experience. The more initials a person used while chatting, the more experience she likely had. Over time, Eileen had become familiar with the online world's unique language. She knew phrases like 'laughing out loud' (LOL), 'be right back' (BRB), and similar shorthand terms that people commonly used when chatting.

Eileen was spending this night in one of the chat rooms designated for locals from Detroit. Though she had never been to Detroit and had no ties to the city, she enjoyed hopping around Cyberspace while tucked away in the comfort of her anonymity, getting to know novel individuals from all walks of life. At times, hanging out in the chat rooms gave her the feeling of listening in on someone else's phone conversations. She also came to believe that chatting anonymously online allowed her to be herself more easily, and for two chatting partners to get to know the *real* person, which often gets masked in real life interactions. How you look or how you dress or how you talk didn't factor into the judgments others might make about you, and therefore these "friendships" were, on some level, *more* sincere and honest, she reasoned.

A window suddenly opened on her computer screen, accompanied by tinkling chimes, indicating a message was being sent directly to her and not to the general audience of the chat room. This was not uncommon, but the question was; and it felt different to her for some reason.

"Hey Cheeryl, my name is Sweetdude35 and it's a pleasure to meet you. Is this as boring to you as it is to me?"

The typical questions from men online were about sex; most men wanted to know whether you were game for chatting sexually, or they'd just dive right into asking for naked pictures. *I wonder where he's headed with this?*

"Do I know you?" she replied.

"No. Just looking for someone to chat with," he answered simply.

"And what does 'Sweetdude35' mean?" she asked, wondering how many more exchanges this chat would go before he asked how big her breasts were.

"Just what it says. I'm sweet, I'm a guy, and I'm 35. How old are you?" he asked.

How old am I? Is that all he wants to know? The apparent sincerity of his replies was startling to her. This wasn't usual, at least not for a guy questioning a woman.

She hesitated, sat back in her chair and looked for her cigarettes and lighter. The rain was falling harder now, and glancing up she noticed one of the windows had been left open and rain was splashing onto the back of the couch. She stood, stretched briefly, and then walked over to close it. It was jammed, but just as she managed to pull it down she turned and froze.

"Oh my god you scared me!" she blurted out, placing her hand flat across her chest as her shoulders hunched up.

"I'm going up. You still working?" asked Ron, standing in the doorway.

"The rain was coming through the window and it was jammed," she said.

"Well it's not now. Are you coming up or not, because I'm shutting the lights off down here."

"I'm not done yet."

"Typing up something on one of those crazies?" he asked, wagging his head and rolling his eyes in an attempt to caricature her patients. "I don't want to disturb your concentration," he said with a smirk. "Why don't you just get this crap done at work?"

"I know, nothing I do could possibly be as important as what you do, right?"

"Whoa, a little defensive, aren't we?"

"Oh come on, Ron, listen to the way you talk about it—"

"Look, just forget it. Are you coming up now or not?" he asked.

"I'll be up later. I'm almost done. Do you need anything before I come up?" she asked, reverting to her typically subservient manner, which usually helped to avoid an argument or kept her distracted from the anger simmering within her.

"No, I'm fine. Goodnight. I'll be out of here early tomorrow morning and then I'm coming home late. And hey, if it stops raining before you come up, why don't you open a window? You're stinking up this place with that smoke."

Their eyes hardly met as they each strained to make conversation. He left the room, and she sat back down at the computer. Sweetdude35 had filled her screen with line after line of, "Hello? You still there? Was it something I said? brb. O.K., I'm back. You there? Where did you go?? Hello."

She put out her cigarette and typed, "I'm back. You there?"

"What happened? I thought you left me. I was just starting to feel the chemistry between us?" said Sweetdude35.

She smiled to herself. "Chemistry? We hardly know each other. What chemistry are you feeling?"

"Aw, come on. You left me hanging here."

"I went to close the window and then my husband walked in. No big deal. I'm still here."

"Ah, you have a husband. You didn't tell me that."

"You didn't ask. Is there anything else you'd like to know?" she asked, thoroughly enjoying the lighthearted, flirtatious back-and-forth.

Surprisingly, he still seemed uninterested in the base conversations that typified many of her previous chat experiences with men.

"Actually, I have a husband, but I don't have a husband," she offered.

"Are you one of those sports widows?" he asked.

"No, he's not into sports. He's just not into me," she shared.

"How long are you married?" he pressed further.

"Hmmm....getting a bit personal, now, aren't we?" she asked, though her teasing and inviting tone could not be captured by the typed words alone.

"I'm sorry. Don't bite my head off. No big deal. I don't need to know your personal problems," he added quickly. "I was married five years myself, actually. Maybe the worst five years of my life. I know exactly what it's like to suffer in a bad marriage. The day of my divorce was the happiest day of my life. I felt like a new man."

"So, you're a single man looking to meet women online, right?" she asked, still skeptical about his motives, but intrigued by his openness and simplicity. She was guarded, but willing to play along.

"I don't meet women online. You never know what kind of wackos you might meet. Don't you read the newspapers?"

"Wackos? Who you calling a wacko?" she teased.

"Honestly, I'm just looking to make friends, and you seem very honest and sweet," he answered.

She felt herself drawn by his flattery, which she knew couldn't be in response to anything she was saying or doing—they'd hardly shared anything! This was ridiculous, she thought. It was artificial, superficial. These interactions lacked visual cues, body language, voice tone and inflection—all of which her therapy training had taught were important for providing a context to reading a person. Yet, here she was enjoying it. Was she getting to *know* the *real* Sweetdude35? Or was this just some guy's obviously transparent attempts to hook her. For what? Probably phone sex, or to meet her in person, or to get off by chatting dirty with her, she thought.

Eileen was a hungry person, though. Love may be blind, but emotional neediness doesn't do a bad job of impairing one's senses either. Besides, she knew this meant nothing. It was for fun— entertainment. She was using him just as he might be using her. It didn't matter. She was being talked to in a way that she hadn't been talked to in years; and she loved it.

She spotted the time in the lower right corner of the computer. "Oh wow! Is it really midnight already?"

"Yes it is. Time to get to bed, don't you think?"

"You're on eastern time too?" she asked.

"Hey, what happened to keeping this anonymous and not getting too personal," he joked. "Just teasing you. But yes, it's midnight here too. Will you be on again tomorrow?"

Eileen's feelings had wavered back and forth through their conversation. She felt alive and free to express herself and at times to vent complaints, but she also felt fleeting moments of guilt as well as a peculiar, hard-to-describe feeling evoked by a realization of what she was doing: sitting alone in her study, late at night, typing away on her keyboard to some stranger. His last question unnerved her. *Will I be on again tomorrow? Why?* Are we supposed to get together again? she wondered. These momentary reflections were pushed aside as she quickly tapped out her last sentence to

Sweetdude35: "I'll talk to you tomorrow," she wrote, ending their conversation with an agreement to his offer.

It was over. She shut down the computer and left the study not wanting to see any further responses, or to reconsider or clarify what she said. Done. It was over. She was going to bed. Who cares what he thinks of her abrupt departure, she thought—this wasn't real; it was just for fun.

If only real life were that easy. Hit the shut down button and the situation you find yourself in just vanishes; tomorrow you can start all over again. That's the way it was with online relationships. This was just fantasy. Or so she thought. Eileen would soon learn that the difference between online and real life relationships was not quite the same as the difference between fantasy and reality. For her patients, fantasy sometimes intruded on reality. For Eileen, reality was about to intrude on fantasy.

Chapter Two

T HE RAIN HAD STOPPED BY MORNING, AND SUNSHINE REACHED completely across the sky for the first time in three days. Eileen washed up, grabbed a bagel and headed for work. Ron had already left, as usual. They hadn't shared breakfast or even faced each other in the morning in well over a month. It's not that they were angry at one another for something specific today; they tended to float unpredictably in and out of these phases where they lived like tenants sharing a common dwelling.

Milltown Community Mental Health Center was an outpatient facility serving three counties. There was an emergency room and psychiatric inpatient floor in the adjoining hospital. Like many of the other therapists at the Center, Eileen was frustrated and disillusioned by the influence of managed health care on her work. More and more of what had been a fulfilling career helping others had transformed into a grinding job, filled more with worries about completing proper documents than about the quality of patient care.

Eileen stopped at the cafeteria for a cup of coffee and ran into Michelle, a psychologist who had been an intern just two years ago. She appeared older than her age—which was actually somewhere in her late twenties—and was still fresh with enthusiasm and none of the cynicism that had infected many of her older colleagues. She was a stocky woman with blonde hair, and pale, whitish skin. A pair of large framed glasses dangled from a chain around her neck. She rarely wore makeup but always dressed impeccably and had her nails done weekly.

Michelle was considered an excellent therapist, particularly with adolescents struggling with addiction, but there was an awkwardness to her social behavior that turned off many of her colleagues. She asked too many questions, expressed too many opinions, and never knew when to leave. Nevertheless, it may very well have been her matronly appearance and strong views that conveyed hope, empathy, and comfort to the troubled adolescents she counseled.

"Are you headed up to the office?" asked Michelle.

"Yes, as soon as I put this change away. How was your weekend?" asked Eileen.

In contrast to her colleagues, Eileen liked Michelle a lot. She liked her enduringly positive outlook on life, on work, and on her patients. They occasionally socialized after work, and Michelle was the only one at work that Eileen felt comfortable speaking to about her marital problems.

"It was good, except for the rain we had this weekend? How was yours?" asked Michelle, looking carefully from the corner of her eyes at Eileen's reaction.

"It was nice. So what's Tim doing about the basement?"

"Eileen?" Michelle blurted in a hushed but still loud voice.

Eileen looked straight ahead and kept walking while Michelle shuffled sideways, carefully holding her coffee to avoid a spill and staring with raised eyebrows directly at Eileen.

"What? What's the matter?" asked Eileen.

"Forget about my basement. What's happening? What happened on Friday?" asked Michelle, trying her best to force her expression of disbelief into Eileen's field of vision.

"Friday?" said Eileen, with an unconvincing puzzled look.

"Eileen, come on. Yes, Friday."

"You know what, Mich, I am really, really sorry. It's like when I left here I was on automatic pilot and I completely—"

"Eileen, Eileen, no," Michelle interrupted. "I'm not concerned about why we couldn't meet for dinner—that's not what I'm asking." Then she stopped and placed her hand on Eileen's shoulder to grab her full attention.

"Michelle," said Eileen, looking with surprise first at Michelle's hand then at her face.

"Eileen, seriously."

"Oh Michelle, talking about it doesn't make it any better," she said as she twisted herself from Michelle's grasp.

"Thank you, Miss Therapist. Is that what you tell your patients?"

They walked into Eileen's office and sat down with their coffees. "Are you going to get some counseling?" Michelle continued.

"I don't know," Eileen repeated several times and then sighed. "He could care less. He thinks what therapists do is...well, it doesn't matter what he thinks because he'd never go."

"Eileen, I'm not talking about marital counseling. I'm talking about you. I'm concerned about *you*."

"You know what, Michelle? I appreciate you caring about me. Let's just not talk about him now. I have a case to present, and I need to have my head clear."

"The Pagnotti case?" asked Michelle.

"How'd you guess?" she replied sarcastically. "This guy is such a...I don't know...Maybe that's my problem."

"What's that?"

"I'm too involved with these cases. That's why my head's not where it should be."

"Eileen, this is the last time. I know you want me to shut up. It's not your patients, you know? It's your husband, and you need to talk to someone."

"Why some stranger when I have you, Michelle. You're my therapist," said Eileen with a smile.

"Eileen, I'm serious—"

"Goodbye, Michelle," said Eileen, and she thanked her with a hug before sweeping her out of the office. "I need to go through my notes. We'll talk later, okay?"

With Eileen standing behind the door, now just about four inches ajar, they continued talking for a few minutes more. Eileen had a hard time ending conversations with Michelle, especially when they talked about her marital problems. Michelle was rather voyeuristic, Eileen thought, and often overstepped the boundaries of their friendship with her prodding and prying. She seemed to deal with everyone as if they were a patient. Eileen finally closed the door.

Monday mornings at nine-thirty the outpatient team gathered in the conference room for a staff meeting. All new patients were presented and discussed among the team members, which included psychiatrists, social workers, psychology interns, psychologists, and masters level counselors. In addition to presenting new patients, staff were free to discuss with the team any patients they wanted help with, particularly those considered high risk.

Dr. Diane Thomas, a psychologist and the staff's supervisor, opened the meeting with several announcements about scheduling conflicts involving the support staff, the need for more intake appointments, and a variety of other mundane matters. The staff routinely ignored this part of the meeting as they surreptitiously caught up on paperwork.

"And the last item," announced Dr. Thomas, "it is imperative— and I'm serious about this—that you make your vacation requests as far in advance as possible. But just because you ask for the time doesn't guarantee you'll get it." She paused, scanned the staff's reactions with her head still and her eyes darting back and forth.

"I need to know who's planning to take off the Thursday or Friday before the Labor Day weekend. We can't be left without staff on those days," she finally concluded. "Okay, let's talk about cases. And please, don't start talking about cases without telling us what kind of insurance the patient has."

"I need to talk about Pagnotti," said Eileen before anyone had a chance to look up from their notes.

"Oh God, him again?" said one of the social workers.

"Yes," continued Eileen. "I don't feel comfortable with what he's saying, but he knows exactly what to say to keep himself from being committed."

"Eileen, please?" Dr. Thomas sighed. Eileen stared at her. "The insurance, Eileen? What insurance does he have? I just finished—"

"Okay, okay, right, I'm sorry. He's got Colsal Healthcare, I think."

"He's manipulating you, Eileen," offered Jeremy, one of the psychology interns.

"Fine, so he's manipulative. I'm still stuck with having him say these things, like he might go home and drink cleaning fluid, or that he feels like cutting himself—"

"I'm sorry, Eileen, you didn't tell us how many sessions he's authorized?" interrupted Dr. Thomas.

"Diane, I'm not sure. I'd have to look that up, but I think he rolled over in July, so he's okay," answered Eileen, then after a quick rolling of her eyes at Dr. Thomas's questioning, turned to the rest of the staff, "Do I just ignore these things because we're saying he's being manipulative? That's it? So I document these statements, and then what happens if one day he decides to actually act on this stuff? Then what?" Eileen shook her head and tossed the chart onto the table in front of her.

"Why don't you take him at his word?" asked Dr. Thomas, giving her "words have consequences" advice again. "Every time he makes reference to wanting to hurt himself or someone else, you walk him over to the emergency room and have him evaluated for possible admission. Let him go through that whole procedure again and again if you have to."

"Also, you're giving him the message that you're taking his feelings seriously, that you care about him," added one of the social workers in agreement.

"Well, for one thing, when push comes to shove he backs off this stuff, and he knows exactly what to say. He literally says, 'I'm not intending to do anything. I can stay safe...for now.' He's been through this so much, he knows exactly what he's doing." said Eileen, drifting into a monotone, her eyes focused nowhere in particular. She sat back and slumped down in her seat, her arms dangling over the sides.

"I think he enjoys controlling you like this," said one of the psychologists. "You know he gets a kick out of what he's doing."

"Well, I'd just feel more comfortable if there was some consensus on how to handle these kinds of situations. I just don't know what to do," she whined. "You know, I don't usually feel like this...with guys like him...but I really *don't like* this guy. I don't have any empathy for him."

Brock Pagnotti, in his forties, divorced and living with his father, was tall and spidery, with arms that dangled off his spare frame. Thick, dark hair cluttered his head, and whether he was seen early in the morning or late in the day, the beard on his colorless face looked like a film of soot, as if he needed to wipe rather than shave. Despite his poor hygiene, he usually dressed well, though he reminded Eileen of a young boy swimming awkwardly in his first suit.

In dress slacks, shirt sleeves, a jacket and tie, Brock arrived without fail to all his sessions. The inconsistency between his personal hygiene and his clothing was both striking and puzzling to Eileen. She always wanted to comment on this, or compliment him on his attire in an effort to prompt a change in his other self-care habits; but she knew better than to remark on his appearance as he would surely misinterpret or sexualize her comments.

"Does he live alone, Eileen?" asked one of the social workers.

"Well, he's living with his father so he can...'take care' of him," said Eileen, quoting her sarcasm with her fingers.

There was no way, Eileen believed, that Mr. Pagnotti had any need for a person like his son to care for him. Even in his seventies, the elder Pagnotti appeared physically fit and was more mentally alert than Brock.

In response to a suggestion that she include Brock's father in the therapy, Eileen explained that Mr. Pagnotti had accompanied his son to several earlier sessions, which deteriorated into bickering and name calling, and now he refused to attend. Brock called his father 'useless' and 'overcontrolling,' while Mr. Pagnotti's pleas for his son to find a job were heard as 'lazy' by Brock.

Brock hadn't kept a job for more than one or two months for at least the last ten years. But as much as his father was fed up with him, Brock never had to worry about his father's financial support.

"Why does he put up with him?" asked a psychiatrist.

Eileen described how Brock's mother had been overbearing and verbally abusive to Brock, an only child, almost from the day he was born. There was no doubt he contributed to their stormy relationship. He was an aggressive, argumentative, and impulsive child who was a terror in school. He received poor grades and had few friends. "Mrs. Pagnotti committed suicide when Brock was fifteen. She hanged herself in the basement, and it was Brock who discovered her body.

"He hated how she treated him and how she made him feel about himself," Eileen explained.

But Brock's hatred was tempered by guilt after his mother's suicide. His father had an unspoken way of implying that Brock's unruliness was a major reason his mother killed herself. This feeling was cemented when Brock was sent to live with his grandmother a year later. Mr. Pagnotti reasoned that he was incapable of caring properly for the child and wanted him in a stable household with a loving woman after all he'd been through. He felt this would give his son a fresh start in his young life.

"I'm sure he saw that as just another rejection, pure and simple, right?" said the psychiatrist.

"Bingo," said Eileen.

After failing at a series of jobs, three hospitalizations to detox from alcohol, and brief jail time for hitting a police officer on the head with a bottle during a fight, Brock, then twenty-six, landed back at home with his father.

"So his father blames himself for having abandoned his son, and feels partly to blame for his son's problems. So there's no way he's kicking him out again," said Eileen to a roomful of attentive listeners.

Although many of the staff had heard this story before, they still found the dynamics interesting, especially the fact that Mr. Pagnotti was resigned to living the remainder of his life suffering with the ambivalence of wanting to rid his life of "this waste of a human being," while pledging never again to desert his only child. Close to twenty years later, the two were still living with each other.

The discussion of Eileen's patient continued with little constructive input from the staff. When the meeting ended, Eileen returned to her office to finish some paperwork. She'd see Brock in less than an hour.

Maybe she chose to present Brock at the meetings simply to vent and to elicit sympathy from her colleagues before having to see him. Several therapists had mentioned that simply keeping him out of the hospital for the past year was an indication of how well her treatment had been. Although keeping someone out of the hospital did not exactly feel like progress, Eileen appreciated those comments. There were times when others offered such definitive suggestions about what she *should* be doing that it felt like criticism. Brock was clearly a difficult patient. Whether he was manipulative or not, and whether or not he enjoyed—in some bizarre way—pushing Eileen's patience to the limit, he was very simply a sick individual, and something needed to be done.

When the phone rang, Eileen reflexively looked up from her notes to check the time; it was eleven o'clock exactly. She let it ring several times, wishing she could fastfoward over the next hour.

"Your eleven o'clock is here, Eileen."

"Thank you, Mary," she said to the receptionist.

Eileen straightened her desk as carefully and deliberately as she could, as if buying precious seconds off Brock's therapy hour, then left her room to greet him and bring him back to her office.

"Mr. Pagnotti?" called Eileen, stretching a smile as best she could. Brock's eyes remained averted. He stood and followed her, huffing through his nostrils to ensure Eileen understood the mood he was in today.

Eileen's office had no windows and just two chairs. She had a small bookshelf, and the walls were adorned with several prints she had brought from home. She pulled her chair away from her desk, which faced the wall that was even with the door. The second chair was situated between the side of her desk and the door. Pagnotti dropped himself hard into the chair, sat stiffly with arms and ankles crossed, and now glared at Eileen.

"I'm a pain in the ass, aren't I?" he barked, his eyes bulging. "I mean, I must be, otherwise why would ya ignore my calls? I'm either a pain in the ass or ya don't take my feelings very seriously or you're just too damn busy. Now, which is it, Doc? Hmmm? Which?"

"Okay, let's slow down one second and relax," said Eileen, steadying herself for the current installment of Brock's rage.

"Relax! Yeah, I'm gonna fuckin' relax. Is that what ya learn to tell your patients, Doc, relax? It's all so simple, right? Just relax and everything is better? Well it's not gonna be better. Will it be better when I'm dead? That's what you're hopin' for, isn't it? When I'm dead then you don't have to see that 'Pagnotti guy' again, that 'pain in the ass.'"

"Are you thinking about hurting yourself, Brock?" asked Eileen. She leaned forward, eyebrows drawn together.

"Ya know, not only would *you* be better off with me dead, but so would that old, crusty asshole," replied Brock.

"Did something happen between you and your father?"

"Maybe if you'd called me last week, you'd know a little about what's goin' on with me," he replied.

"Brock, I apologize for whatever miscommunication occurred here in our office that caused me to miss your message. But I want you to understand that I care about you. If I had gotten the message I would have called you back—you know that. But right now what I'm most concerned about is you and whether you're going to hurt yourself."

It took a tremendous effort (was it acting or clinical skill, she always wondered) to muster these words in order to convey some sense of empathy for him.

"Are you thinking about hurting yourself?" she persisted.

"I'm not sure," he answered with a pout, his eyes turned away like a sulking child.

This was a typical pattern. He would plunge into references about being dead, which—he knew all too well—forced Eileen to shift immediately into 'highly concerned mode,' asking him about suicidal thoughts and conveying to him how much she cared for his life and her need to protect him from harming himself. If she wasn't caring enough for him, he'd create a crisis to procure every ounce of concern and compassion he could from her (however feigned on her part). For today's crisis, he believed Eileen had slighted him by neglecting to return a phone call he'd made to her at the end of last week.

Deciding on the strategy Dr. Thomas recommended earlier in the staff meeting, Eileen took his words seriously and literally in order to establish the need for hospitalization. She wasn't going to interpret this behavior as an adolescent-like tantrum, or as a means to punish her for her supposed transgression. This contrasted markedly with her previous style, which was to ignore the literal meaning of Pagnotti's suicidal references and instead to focus on whatever disturbed feelings lay beneath his words.

Eileen composed herself and continued, "Brock, are you saying that when you leave here today you don't know if you can control these impulses to hurt yourself?"

"What I'm saying is, who the fuck do ya think y'are? What kind of place is this? I could have offed myself last week! But would you have known it? No! You don't return phone calls," he shouted, his anger showing no signs of letting up.

"Brock, I told you that there was a mix up here and I apologize for that. I care about you, and what I want to know now is if it's safe for you to leave here today."

"Why would ya care if it's safe—"

"Brock, you're not answering my question," she declared, cutting him off.

"And what question is that?" he asked, his head cocked to the side as he peered at Eileen with suspicion.

"Are you thinking now about hurting yourself?"

"I'm not sure. Maybe I am," he said, eyes fixed on his hands as he rubbed his fingers and cracked his knuckles.

"You know what, Brock? I'm concerned about you. I don't want you hurting yourself. Do you think you need to be in a hospital to stay safe?"

"A hospital? Are you fucking nuts?" he scoffed. He stopped playing with his fingers and squinted at Eileen.

"Brock, I'm not having you leave here today with the feelings you're having," she replied, and she was prepared to see this through to its conclusion even though this was a typical Pagnotti 'pseudo crisis,' as she liked to call it.

She was confident he wouldn't do anything to hurt himself; he never did. But if he was going to use provocative language with her, she was prepared to make him pay for it. She was delighting in this new found sense of power and control. She was no longer providing therapy, though; she was meting out his punishment like a mother asking her son to open his mouth while she washed it out with soap for using dirty words.

"I'm not going to do anything right now, ya know. That's not what I'm saying," insisted Pagnotti, now backing off his earlier statements.

"I'm concerned about how you're feeling, and I don't think you can just turn something like that on and off, Brock. You may not like the idea of being in the hospital, but why don't we at least get a second opinion."

Brock sat in the waiting room while Eileen made several phone calls searching for a psychiatrist to give a second opinion, which was necessary if Pagnotti were to be involuntarily committed. Even though she had to cancel and move around several appointments, and the ordeal with Pagnotti moved into its third hour, Eileen seemed revitalized by the actions she was taking. She felt she'd turned the tables on him this time. He'd come in like a spoiled brat, she thought, and was going to rip her apart with his rage and his threats until he received what he considered to be an adequate apology. Instead she'd ignored the meaning—his feelings of rejection—and zeroed in on the literal meaning of his words.

Accompanied by security, she finally walked Pagnotti to the psychiatric emergency room next door, where registration alone took another forty-five minutes. After giving clinical information to the attending psychiatrist, Dr. Williams, Eileen returned to her office feeling spent but satisfied. She asked Dr. Williams to let her know whether Pagnotti went voluntarily or had to be committed to another hospital.

Michelle was waiting in the secretary's office when Eileen returned. "What happened with Pagnotti?"

"Guess where he is right now?" answered Eileen, unable to suppress her glee.

"No way!"

"Yep. He's been here close to five hours now. We hardly had a session. He started right in about some phone call I didn't return, and he starts talking about how he could be dead and I wouldn't even know it because I don't return calls and so on and on and on. It was his usual performance," said Eileen with a smirk and a wink.

"So what did you do? He's going inpatient?"

"Yep."

"Voluntary?"

"I don't know. I doubt it. He nearly fell off his chair when I mentioned the hospital to him," she laughed. "The psychiatrists weren't around so I had to walk him next door. He's being evaluated now. I think he's committable, but even if he doesn't go inpatient he's going to think twice about what he says in the future."

"He's going to be pissed, you know?" said Michelle.

"So he's pissed. How's that going to be any different. I really don't care how he feels," said Eileen.

"Eileen. I know he's a pain in the ass, but this isn't you. You sound as if...as if...you just wanted to punish him."

"This is exactly what Dr. Thomas was talking about," Eileen shot back, her tone rising. Her smile left and she scanned Michelle's expression for the slightest sign of disagreement.

Michelle shook her head. "I don't know, Eileen. He's a difficult patient, but this is what we get paid to do. Lately you just sound so...so...I don't know, fed up with everything."

Eileen felt her face getting flush and sensed her pulse beating in her head, but she clenched her teeth and said nothing.

They walked back to Michelle's office and sat down to talk some more. They were interrupted a short time later by the phone. Michelle answered and handed it to Eileen.

"It's Dr. Williams."

"Hi, Dr. Williams...Oh, you're kidding. Are you serious? But he always says that. He knows that's what he needs to say to keep out of the hospital...I know...I know...No...That's true...You know what? You need to call back to set that up with one of the secretaries...Yes, I'm sure I have something open by Friday."

Eileen alternated between standing and sitting while she talked, shifting around in her seat, slapping a hand on her head and rolling her eyes to dramatize her frustration to Michelle, who looked on with a continuous bobbing and shaking of her head and a loathsome expression that told Eileen she knew exactly what the conversation was about.

She finished and handed the phone back to Michelle who hung it up without removing her eyes from Eileen.

"He went home, right?" asked Michelle.

Eileen's reply was a derisive, sing-song recitation of Dr. Williams's rationale: "'They couldn't commit him, he contracted for safety, he promised he wouldn't hurt himself, he's feeling much better now, he agreed to a follow up appointment, they can't see committing him and there's no way he was going voluntarily.'" She sat down in a chair and slid forward to allow her head to lean against the back. "Now I have to face him *again* this week," she pouted.

"Eileen, you can't solve your problems by taking your anger out on your patients," said Michelle, offering her analysis as tactfully as she could.

"Michelle! This isn't about Ron and me," said Eileen, looking at the floor. "Stop trying to analyze me, please! And stop relating everything to my personal life. I...I...I'm sorry...I should never have confided in you. You're...you're...Oh, forget it." Eileen sprung from her chair and pushed her way passed Michelle and out the door.

"Eileen, I'm not analyzing you—" she called out, but Eileen was gone.

She knew Michelle was right but detested being told how she thought and how she felt. What Michelle considered support or helpful advice often bordered on intrusive. At times like this it was downright unbearable, she thought.

Exhausted and distracted, Eileen finished for the day and hurried quietly from the office. When she arrived home, she noticed her sister's car in the driveway. Ron was home too—early—which was amazing, she thought. What was he up to, she wondered.

Chapter Three

K ELLY AND RON STOPPED TALKING AND LOOKED AT EILEEN AS SHE entered the kitchen.

"Oh God, Leenie, you look wiped," said Kelly, taking a few steps away from Ron and turning toward her sister. Ron opened a drawer looking for nothing in particular and then went to the sink for a glass of water.

"How did you get in?" asked Eileen.

"Ron was here; he let me in. Eileen, you should see this awesome, awesome—"

"Did I miss something? Is it someone's birthday?" asked Eileen, dropping herself into a chair.

"No, we...Ron and I...I was stopping by to see you and say 'hi' and Ron was here, and we thought it might be cool if we all went out for a bite," said Kelly, looking at Ron for his corroboration.

"Kel got a babysitter," said Ron.

"Out to eat? I'm too beat," said Eileen. "How about we just eat in."

"And eat what?" snapped Ron, opening and slamming shut a nearly empty cabinet to make his point.

"So if I don't go shopping, we can't eat?"

"That's not what I'm saying, Eileen. You twist everything. Did it ever occur to you to do something on the spur of the moment?

How about a little spontaneity? Hmmm? My God!" he shouted, glaring at Eileen from across the kitchen.

Kelly looked at Ron then at Eileen and through a thin smile offered, "Ummm, why don't we do this another night?"

"No, Kelly, just...can you go into the other room, please?" asked Ron.

"Come on, Ronnie, let's just forget it. It's no biggie if we skip tonight. You guys need to—"

"Kelly, please! Just step into the living room for two seconds, all right?" Ron implored.

"No, look, I don't want to ruin the night. You don't have to send her into the other room," Eileen said to Ron. "I had a God-awful day with a difficult patient, and I'm just not in a mood to go out. We don't need to talk. Why don't the two of you just go without me. I'll be all right. I'll make something for myself later, after I rest a bit."

"Let's just go, Kelly," Ron grunted, grabbing his keys and marching toward the door.

Kelly placed a hand on Eileen's shoulder, leaned forward and whispered, "I'll call you tomorrow. Get some rest, okay?" She kissed her on the head, swirled around and left the kitchen.

When they were outside, Kelly turned to Ron and asked, "What's going on with her?"

"Oh please, Kel, I haven't a clue," said Ron, swatting his hand disgustedly in the direction of the house. "There's nothing wrong with her; that's just *her*. She's been like this for awhile, and I'm not about to stand around trying to figure her out—I give up. She's the therapist. She ought to be figuring herself out. His face now softening and eyes pleading, he asked, "Can we not talk about her and just enjoy dinner? Where do you want to go?"

"Let's go to the Mexican place in Brookridge."

"Separate cars?"

"Yessiree. It'll be easier for me to just leave from there."

Both shot quick glances at the house, scanning for a face in the window or Eileen at the door, then turned to each other and kissed. They smiled at each other, then snuggled in each other's arms before getting into their cars and driving off.

Kelly was two years younger than Eileen, but it seemed more like fifteen years between them. She was pretty, with green eyes and thick, dark hair that unfurled down her back, her slender frame mirroring her youthful spirit. It was this spirit that grabbed Ron's interest. He was attracted to her shifting moods, her impulsiveness, her playfulness, her willingness to change plans on a whim. In contrast, Eileen was planful, almost rigid. And where Eileen was burdened by ceaselessly seeking to appease others, Kelly's assertiveness—at times bordering on brazenness—presented an air of self-confidence and unpredictability that Ron found invigorating.

Eileen wondered—but couldn't bring herself to ask—why Kelly would still go out after witnessing the tension between her and Ron. She didn't want to start trouble. There was a lot she wanted to ask about, but she didn't want a scene with Ron blowing up in front of her sister and slamming more than cabinets. She kept her questions to herself to keep the peace.

After they left, Eileen heated some leftover pasta and sat down in front of the computer to surf the Internet. After browsing some headline news, she logged onto her chat program. Within thirty seconds a window on the screen popped up. It was a chat message from Sweetdude35.

"Hey Cheeryl, long time, no chat."

Startled, she asked, "How did you know I was on?"

"I added you to my list. So whenever you log on, your name blinks and I know you're there," said Sweetdude35.

"I didn't even think about that. I guess I should add your name to my list, right?"

"Well I certainly think you should, but I'm biased because I think you're really sweet."

"Well, flattery will get you nowhere tonight, Mr. Sweet talker. I had a bad day."

"What kind of work do you do?" asked Sweetdude35.

Eileen paused. Should she tell him she's a therapist? She turned away from the computer and distracted herself with some pasta. How much should she reveal about herself? She felt comfortable with him mainly because he didn't talk dirty to her, and because he *seemed* sincere. These were not stellar reasons to trust someone you knew only by a nickname—and a nickname like *Sweetdude35* no less. She thought about how awkward it was in real life to reveal she was a therapist—the standard reply usually being, "Oh, so are you analyzing me?"

After a few forkfuls of pasta were washed down with wine while she mulled over these issues, she decided to share some information. Instead of making an issue of her privacy concerns by refusing to answer, she decided to bend the truth a little. Rather than having to deal with questions about *analyzing* him or about what kinds of *kooks* she deals with, she decided to tell him she was a teacher.

"A teacher, eh. What do you teach?" he continued.

"It doesn't matter. Put it this way. I had a bad day with a student," she replied.

"Where's your hubby tonight."

"He's out. And let's not go there either."

"Ah, a marriage gone sour."

"I didn't say that. I just don't want to talk about it."

"Sometimes talking about it helps. Even if there's no immediate solution to the problem. At least that's what my therapist tells me."

Eileen nearly choked on her wine. "Your *therapist*?"

"Hey, I'm giving you too much personal stuff now, right? Forget I said that. I don't want you to think I'm some nut," said Sweetdude35.

"No no no. That's O.K. Lot's of people are in therapy. I think that's good, and I think it's great that you feel comfortable sharing that. The truth is, I could probably use some therapy myself, or at least for my marriage."

She put her fork down and shoved the bowl and glass away. She wriggled her seat closer to the computer and sat upright. Suddenly this was a conversation of substance, she thought.

"Well, why don't you try it? Have you asked him?"

"He thinks therapy is bullshit."

"Sometimes if you go yourself and show him you're getting help for your problems, he might be willing to join later on."

"Are you sure *you're* not a therapist?" asked Eileen. Her eyes were wide as she stared at the words on her screen. She smiled as she grew more comfortable opening up to him.

"Can I tell you something?" she continued. "This is the most I've opened up to someone in a long time."

And she thought once again it was because it's anonymous—it's easier being your true self this way.

"Opened up? You call this opening up? You've hardly told me anything. When do we get to the juicy part?" teased Sweetdude35.

"Well, there really isn't any juicy part. He and I just don't click anymore."

"How long have you been married?"

"Ten years. But we've known each other since high school."

"Since high school, eh. How long is that?"

"Close to thirty years or so. There was a time in the middle there where we didn't see each other. But we should be closer. We should be best friends, but we're not."

"Any kids?"

"No kids. We sort of, or I guess we sort of agreed on that from the beginning."

As they continued chatting, she revealed more and shared more of herself, but when she asked him questions, he usually brought the conversation back to her.

"How about you? You have any kids?" she asked.

"Nope. So what happened today with the student?"

"Student?" she asked, forgetting her earlier lie.

"You said you had a bad day with a student. What happened? How old are the kids you teach?"

"High school. You know how spoiled some of these kids can be." She scrolled back on her computer screen to refresh her memory about what she'd told him earlier. She grinned as she re-read her analogy: switching therapist for teacher and student for patient.

"He's just some guy who's a big pain in my ass and I wish he'd go away. I literally feel sick when I come home. I just don't know how to deal with him. And then when I come home, I've got my own problem to deal with," she continued.

"Can't you have him moved to another class? Is he dangerous or something?"

"*Dangerous?* That's a pretty strong word. I don't know...maybe...I suppose you could say I wouldn't want to run into him in a dark alley. But you can't just move students around like that and dump them on some other teacher," explained Eileen.

"So what does hubby do when you're online? Is he around?" asked Sweetdude35, returning back to the topic of her husband.

"My husband is out and I really don't care. Even if he were home, we wouldn't be talking to each other."

"That's sad. I feel bad for you," said Sweetdude35.

"Thank you," she replied, and her eyes were moist. There was a pause for a minute.

"You still there?" said Sweetdude35, finally breaking their inactivity.

"I'm here," replied Eileen.

She was feeling emotional. The tears that had swelled now trickled toward her lips. She wanted to discuss her feelings, and her failing marriage, and the stress at work, but she never had any outlet. Even when she confided in Michelle, she hid the intensity of her feelings along with much of the details. But somehow, simply typing away on the computer to a stranger—and a very sympathetic stranger at that—was cathartic. And it was anonymous, too. He didn't know her, just as she didn't know him. In a way, it was almost like writing your thoughts in a diary or journal. Except here you get a response, which made it that much better. And he seemed so *insightful*, she thought.

"We used to spend so much time together. After work, we always made sure we were together for dinner. And he always had so much to say about his work, and I'd tell him about my work. You know? We were buddies," she started spilling to Sweetdude35. "He cared about what I said and the opinions I had about his work. But now it's like we're strangers. No feelings. And No communication. When we do try to talk, it always ends up with him getting angry."

"I'm sorry to hear that," he sympathized. "It sounds like things have really changed."

"I hear about this all the time. I'm the one who has to deal with this at work. And it's always easier to deal with a problem when it's someone else's," said Eileen, and then she realized she was mixing up her facts and neglecting the teacher analogy she was using to protect her privacy.

"I thought these were high school students???" asked Sweetdude35, using a string of question marks to underscore how puzzled he was over her last remark.

Pausing, Eileen re-read her last statement, then clarified, "A lot of the students' parents have problems that they share with the teachers. You know, being a teacher is like being a bartender; people share their problems with you."

"I'm not exactly sure I know what's going on," said Sweetdude35, and pressing for more details, asked, "what is wrong? Does he hit you? Do you think he's sleeping with someone else? Does he drink too much?"

"Whoa! Slow down with the questions—"

"I'm sorry. I'm getting too personal again?"

"No, that's O.K. If I don't want to tell you something, I won't tell you. It's O.K. I'm actually enjoying this. It's not often I get to talk to someone like this. I appreciate you caring. It's funny. We're just typing away here and yet I can really sense that you care."

"I do care, and I think you're really special too. It's a shame he treats you the way he does."

"Slow down, Mr. Sweet Talker. I never said you were 'special.' Don't get all mushy on me," she replied, and she smiled at her teasing response, but he could only read her words unaccompanied by her playful smile.

"Awwww, come on. I'm not special? Don't you feel the chemistry between us," Sweetdude35 persisted.

"I'm teasing. Typing this stuff loses something because you can't see me; I'm just teasing you. You can't hear my tone of voice. I *do* think you're special...in a different kind of way."

"A different kind of way?"

"Yeah. I mean, I don't think I've *ever* had a normal conversation like this online with a guy."

"I guess I am different. In a good way, right?"

"Yes, in a good way. I like talking to you," she said.

"Do you want to talk on the phone sometime?" he asked.

Her neck tightened and she felt flush. The pulse beating inside her head drowned out the hum of the computer. Just a simple question and Eileen immediately understood how anonymous, innocent chatting could insidiously change to something more risky, even dangerous. And yet she felt drawn to this person. He was listening to her and he was caring. Maybe he could listen on the phone, she thought. It might even feel better that way. That's just stupid and crazy, she thought, snapping out of her daze.

In an instant it seemed as if every news story flashed through her mind about a lunatic who meets an innocent victim online and then finds out where the person lives. And wasn't this just a bit too fast? How often had they chatted? Twice, and he's asking to talk on the phone! *What would he do, call me?* Or am I supposed to call *him*, she wondered. *Is he that naïve to think I'd give him my phone number?*

Maybe he'd give out his number and expect me to call. That would be okay, unless he had caller I.D., she thought.

With her thoughts ricocheting into and out of various scenarios—and against her better judgment—she offered Sweetdude35 some hope. She replied to his question about the phone very simply: "Maybe."

She preferred to say no, but didn't want to hurt his feelings.

"Well if it's easier for you, I could call you at work. Or if it would make you feel better, you could call me from your work. That way your husband won't see the number on the phone bill."

Wow, he's persistent, she thought. "I said maybe. That also means maybe not."

"By the way, I don't even know where you live. I know you said you're on eastern time. But any chance you could narrow that down for me?" he asked.

Boy, he's smooth, she thought. Is this just some kind of tricky way of finding out where she lives? Now I'm overdoing it, she thought. *I'm being paranoid. He's been very nice, and all he's doing is asking the general vicinity, not my address.*

Eileen let her feelings lead her and soon discovered that the more she shared with him, the more comfortable she felt divulging personal information, as if her willingness to open up to him were evidence of his trustworthiness.

"I'm along the coast. How's that for narrowing it?" she answered.

"Cool. Me too."

"You are? Are you north or south?" she asked, initiating a pinpointing game with a tinge of uneasiness.

"Have you ever been to New York City?" he asked.

"Yourfrom newyork?" Her typing was fast and sloppy now as her spindly fingers stammered across the keyboard. Each turn of this hot and cold game dragged this online stranger—who just a minute ago was confined solely to text on a screen—a little closer to reality.

He saw only her question about whether he was from New York. Absent from the text was her sense of alarm, along with her widening eyes and trembling fingers.

"Actually, I'm from New Jersey."

She swallowed hard and could feel her face go pale. Suddenly, everything she had confided in this stranger seemed wrong, simply because he was in *her* state. She'd heard of people going online and chatting with strangers from far away places like Australia or Israel or England. It seemed less serious, at least less wrong, that she was sharing her problems with someone who was just "out there" in cyberspace somewhere. Floating out there in cyberspace made him—and what they were doing—less real and less significant. But here he was *in her state,* and that felt wrong.

"You there?" he asked, as she sat staring at the screen.

"I'm here," she managed to type with great effort.

"Where are you from?" he asked, seemingly free of the agony she was experiencing.

"You know," she began, "I think this will work better if we just keep our private lives private. You know how these things can get weird online when people start handing out phone numbers and addresses. I'd just feel more comfortable if I didn't have to say where I'm from. I'm on the east coast, like you, O.K.?"

"Sure, that's fine with me. You're the one who asked if I was north or south, remember?"

"O.K., let's just drop it. Besides, I'm going to bed now, so I need to say goodbye."

"Was it something I said?" he asked.

"No, not at all. I really liked this." And she did, but her hands felt icy and were still trembling.

"This was nice," he said.

"Yes it was. And now I have you on my list, so I'll know when you're online," she said.

"Can I get your email address before you go?" he asked.

Quickly and thoughtlessly, she wrote her email address and sent it with the tag: "Good night, my chat buddy."

He replied with a good night, but she had logged off already. And immediately she began second-guessing her decision to give out her email address. She sat in front of the now quiet and blank computer screen. Why did I do that, she worried, and she held her fists tightly against the sides of her head and grimaced. Oh, it's no big deal, she reasoned. It's not my address or phone number. The worst he could do is harass me with email, in which case I'd change my account. No big deal, she thought, as she calmed herself, and reached for a cigarette.

Finishing her cigarette, she noticed the clock said ten-thirty. She'd been chatting for quite awhile and wondered where Ron and Kelly were. She looked outside and saw both cars were still gone. She thought Kelly might have come back to have coffee afterwards, but now it looked as though she'd go straight home after dinner. Maybe she's home already, and Ron is out alone somewhere avoiding me, she wondered. She picked up the phone to call Kelly, but as she began to dial she heard a car pull in the driveway. It was Ron.

Eileen was sitting on the love seat facing the door when Ron entered the house. He glanced at her then at the coffee table where he tossed his keys. Eileen's stomach was in knots. A number of fragmented thoughts passed through her mind. She hated initiating most kinds of conversation, but she especially disliked those that might hint of a disagreement.

"Can we talk, Ron?" she said just barely above a whisper.

Ron stopped and seemed to glower at her. "Talk? About what?" he asked.

This was difficult for her, but she persisted. "About us," she replied.

"What about us? Now you want to manage my life again?"

"I'm not looking to manage your life. Can't we just have a

conversation, just a normal conversation without all this tension?"
she pleaded.

"I'm not the one creating the tension, Eileen."

"Can we just start over?"

"I don't know where the hell you're going with this, but I'm
going to bed." He hurried passed her and headed for the stairs.

"Ron, just listen to me for a second, please!" she cried as she
jumped from her seat and inserted herself in his path while stepping
backwards as he proceeded down the hallway toward the stairs.

"I'm not listening to this crap, Eileen—" he stopped when he
saw tears streaming down her face.

"I'm so unhappy, Ron. I can't stand the way we're living. I can't
stand this. I want to do something about this...about us!" she cried,
choking on her words as she fought back tears.

He brushed her aside and continued toward the steps yelling
over his shoulder, "I'm not going to talk to you when you start with
that fucking crying, Eileen! I'm supposed to feel sorry for you?"
Then turning around when he reached the foot of the stairs, he
yelled, "You're the victim, right? You cry, so I'm supposed to feel
guilty? Look at the miserable life I make for you, right? Well go to
hell, Eileen!"

He vaulted up the stairs two steps at a time and slammed the
bedroom door behind him.

She had tried to avoid this. She was shaking, her heart was
pounding, and she was hyperventilating. Times like this brought
to mind her father yelling at her mother, and she shuddered at the
thought she could end up married to a man with as much rage as
her father. The thought repulsed her. She considered dropping
the issue—she could sit and wait until he fell asleep. She knew the
problem would wilt if she ignored it. They'd been through this
before, and Ron never had any interest in "working through their
differences," as she put it. "Leave your therapy shit at the office

for the nuts and leave me alone," he'd usually scoff, and then he'd walk away.

But tonight, for whatever reason, she found herself compelled to press this issue further. It occurred to her that she may be pressing this confrontation because of something her online friend, Sweetdude35, had said earlier. Maybe she felt obliged. *Obliged?* He seemed to care. She knew she'd be relaying these events online to him sometime later, probably tomorrow. As unlikely—maybe even crazy—as it seemed, she was propelled by a need to explain herself to Sweetdude35. She felt she had to be able to respond to any question he may have that she could have been more assertive with her husband. It was like feeling the "conscience" or "little voice" that her patients often experienced. They'd sometimes describe their appreciation of, or illustrate the real life effect of her treatment by saying something like, "I wanted to come in here and be able to tell you I *did it*, Eileen. I could hear your voice cheering me on!"

She noticed as she stood at the bottom of the steps, lost in these thoughts, that she was now considerably more composed. As if to seize the eye of the storm, she raced up the stairs to the bedroom.

Upon entering the room she headed straight to Ron's side of the bed, where he lay with remote in hand and eyes gazing at the television. She stepped between him and the television, whirled around and shut it off. Before she could get a word out, Ron had leapt from the bed, baring clenched teeth, and a vein that seemed embossed on his forehead whenever his fury was triggered. In an instant he recoiled his arms toward his shoulders, then thrust his hands forward with his entire weight behind him pounding her chest with a loud *THUD!* The impact lifted her off her feet as she tumbled backward, landing on the floor and shaking the dresser enough to knock over two pictures.

The incident occurred so quickly and unexpectedly that she sat stunned for a minute. Ron had never hit her. A panicky feeling engulfed her as she sat on the floor, humiliated, and feeling like

a little girl. He pushed her! He'd tossed her aside as if she were
nothing to him, a mere annoyance to be flung away. She felt so
ashamed as he ignored her now. She hadn't noticed when, but at
some point he had turned the T.V. back on and returned to his
position on the bed flipping through the channels as if nothing
had happened.

Eileen thinks she walked out of the room and down the stairs,
but didn't remember feeling her feet move; nor did she feel herself
descending the steps. She wasn't crying now, and she wasn't feeling
ashamed or angry or scared. In fact, she felt nothing. It was as if her
emotions had been anesthetized. She was numb. The next thing
she remembered was curling up on the love seat in the living room
and falling asleep.

Chapter Four

K ELLY HAD KNOWN RON SINCE HER SISTER STARTED DATING HIM IN high school. Kelly was a poor student who spent more time partying and less time studying than Eileen. Eileen was the stable, studious one with whom Ron could have an intelligent conversation; but when he wanted sex he turned to Kelly. They began sleeping together when Kelly was a senior in high school and continued until Ron graduated in Kelly's sophomore year of college. Although they frequently developed complicated arrangements to spend time together without Eileen's knowing, it never occurred to them that the real risk was not to Ron and Eileen's high school romance, but to Kelly and Eileen, who, despite their differences, were as close as sisters can be. In short, Kelly was cheating on Eileen.

There was no doubt Ron loved and adored Eileen. And he easily separated the primitive needs he gratified with Kelly from the more mature devotion he felt toward Eileen. It was unnecessary for Kelly to compartmentalize her conflicting behaviors, feelings, and impulses as Ron did. In Ron's mind, he separated the sex he had with Kelly and the relationship he had with Eileen in the same way he separated his work suits from his weekend leisure clothes. By contrast, Kelly lacked the capacity for self-reflection. It wasn't that she acted before thinking; she just acted. Ron avoided guilt with his rationalizations. Kelly avoided guilt by not thinking at all.

Ron was a single child who was raised by adoptive parents in the Bronx since he was nine months old. They moved to New Jersey when Ron entered high school, where he met Eileen within the first week. They bonded immediately. She craved the attention he gave her and welcomed the opportunity their relationship provided to escape the problems she was dealing with at home. Ron had similar family problems, but Eileen never knew about them.

Ron's father was hitting and verbally abusing his wife for as long as Ron could remember, although it never seemed to bother Ron much. It seemed natural to him. Ron's dad, a World War II veteran, didn't beat his wife because he was an alcoholic. No, he was just an angry man on disability since his early thirties due to a severe back injury he suffered when he slipped on the ice getting out of his car one day. The three of them seemed to accept Ron's mother as the guilty party in this mishap (even though her only role in this event was to be present in the passenger's seat). It really didn't take much time—maybe a couple of years—of Ron's father venting anger and frustration that accompanied the lifestyle changes caused by his disability, for the family simply to *believe* that Ron's mother *must* have been the cause of these unfortunate events; otherwise, why would her husband be so mad at her? That seemed logical to all of them, including Ron's mother, who accepted the abuse willingly. The pain she suffered seemed to mitigate her guilt over the accident she didn't cause but was blamed for anyway.

Neither Ron nor Eileen ever talked much about their families, particularly their fathers. Ron kept it to himself because it seemed completely inconsequential. Eileen didn't talk about her father because she couldn't face that it was real. In her mind, talking about it made it real; not talking about it or not thinking about it was liking sticking it in a junk drawer somewhere—out of sight, but never really gone.

As senior year approached, Ron and Eileen grew apart as it became clear they'd be hundreds of miles apart after graduation. Ron was going away to graduate school in Michigan, and Eileen was staying in New Jersey. Rather than causing them to spend as much time together as possible, the inevitable parting actually led to a gradual emotional distancing between them. Ron took a pragmatic, unemotional approach to this: their plans for college led in different directions, so the relationship would have to end. Very neat and simple. It wasn't logical to intensify his attachment when it was going to end anyway, he figured.

For Eileen, the eventual break-up was painful, so she became involved with other activities to distract her from thinking about it. She occupied her time with the Yearbook and the Drama club, and this cut into time she could spend with Ron. So the relationship slowly dissolved in a rather anticlimactic fashion.

Eileen and Ron had no contact until he moved back to New Jersey. By contrast, Kelly spoke often to Ron by phone through those years and met with him on at least a dozen occasions. It was actually Kelly who first met with Ron after he'd completed his MBA and had moved back to New Jersey. Her husband was dying of cancer and Ron's interest in her well-being, together with their easy accessibility to one another led to a rekindling of their mutual lust. Soon they were having sex often. Ron felt he was helping out an old friend. Kelly appreciated the time and effort he put into providing an outlet for the rather horrible circumstances she was facing.

Kelly acted without thinking, and therefore never mentioned to Eileen that Ron had been back in town for six months, just as she had never told her about their other contacts throughout the time he was in Michigan. Ron had put Eileen out of his mind and never considered trying to contact her. But when Ron and Eileen eventually ran into each other, they fell in love again immediately. And, interestingly, neither Ron nor Kelly had trouble resuming their previous roles in this triangle. Ron belonged to Eileen, but

Ron and Kelly slept with each other. And of course, only Eileen was kept in the dark about this. Ron didn't have a relationship with Kelly; he had sex with her.

Ron loved Eileen's intelligence; he also loved that he could talk to her in a way he couldn't talk to Kelly. Yet Kelly provided excitement. But when Ron and Eileen married, Ron began to feel trapped. He felt they married too quickly, though he never mentioned this to Eileen. Spending time with Kelly became more difficult, and the frustration seemed to be just enough to feed a growing resentment toward Eileen. It was as if Eileen was to blame for the fact that Ron couldn't have all his needs so conveniently and immediately met. Ron, of course, learned the importance of scapegoating from his father. Just as his mother was to blame for all his father's ill-will and misery, Eileen soon became the target for Ron's. One major difference between Ron and his father was that Ron never hit his wife. Until now, that is, for Ron had just crossed that line.

When Eileen awoke on the love seat, the soreness that extended down her left shoulder and upper back reminded her of how her life had changed with the events of last night. An emotional recollection seemed to precede a conscious memory of the events. Her body trembled and her stomach felt as if she were being dropped down a chute. She took quick, short breaths as her heart thumped rapidly. When her surroundings seemed to blur, she leapt off the couch and bounded into the bathroom to splash cold water on her face.

She looked in the mirror and her scattered thoughts slowly came together as her mind finally caught up with her emotions: Ron had hit her. He'd pushed her in anger and pushed her hard— hard enough to knock her to the ground. She felt ashamed. She couldn't look at herself anymore.

She walked into the living room and noticed the time on the VCR said eight-thirty. She looked out the window, confirming what she knew: Ron had already left for work. Were they going to talk about this? Would he call her at work to apologize? How should she react? Should she be angry? Forgiving? Would he be remorseful? Or would he act as if nothing happened? That was possible; she knew him well. She also knew that people who have trouble controlling their anger don't usually take any responsibility for what they do or for the consequences of their actions. It's always someone else's fault. He might very well be feeling angry—not guilty—for her *causing* him to push her. After all, she was the one who made him so uncontrollably angry. Yes, that's exactly how he was thinking, she was convinced, and she began to cry.

She managed to shower and dress, then left for work around nine-fifteen without eating breakfast. She stopped at the cafeteria for a cup of coffee, hoping she could avoid running into Michelle. She hastened to her office, looking straight ahead and avoiding eye contact with anyone, as if this somehow concealed her. She couldn't help feeling as if she had a sign on her back that read: "Kick me. Battered Wife here." She felt as though she were on stage, or like a criminal caught on a surveillance camera. As if by reflex, she felt responsible for the failings or destructive acts of others, especially those of Ron.

She stopped briefly in the main office to pick up her daily schedule, then closed herself in her office, relieved.

The phone rang.

"Hi, Eileen, you with someone?" asked Michelle.

"No, I'm just trying to get some paperwork done before—" she stopped while scanning her schedule. "Shit! I have to see Pagnotti today. Can you believe this? Oh, Mich, this sucks."

"Ooooo, he is going to be very pissed at you, Eileen," teased Michelle.

Eileen was quiet for awhile, but then Michelle heard what sounded like sniffling. "Eileen, are you crying?" she asked. "Eileen? I'm joking. Are you okay?"

"I'm okay. I just had a bad night, that's all, and then I'm just...I'm just really stressed out. I'll be okay. I'm not crying—I'm just feeling a little overwhelmed right now."

"Eileen, you should take some time off, really. This is about Ron, isn't it? Are you sure you're okay?"

"I am. Now let me get my act together so I can face this guy."

"When is he coming in?" asked Michelle.

"Two-thirty."

"Let's have lunch together, like around one or so," said Michelle.

"I can't. I have a twelve-thirty. I won't be free till one-thirty."

"Okay, let's do one-thirty, but I'll only have a half-hour because I have a two o'clock patient."

"Okay, I have you penciled in, Michelle. See you then. And thanks again for caring about me," she said, but her voice seemed to drone unconvincingly.

"Eileen, I'm serious!"

"I know you are! I do appreciate it, Mich, I do."

"I just want you to be happy again. You're not yourself."

"I know. I know. Everything will be all right, okay? I have to go. Talk to you later."

Eileen sat in her office not doing much of anything. She stared out the window occasionally. Her eyes tearing often. She attempted to complete some paperwork, but couldn't concentrate. Periodically she felt a wave of anxiety pass through her and she had trouble getting her breath. She knew these were panic attacks and they would pass, but she was becoming increasingly worried they'd occur at an inopportune time when she might be around other people or unable to hide what was happening.

She managed to complete several treatment plans and progress notes and actually made it through a session with an adolescent. When one-thirty rolled around, which was much later than she normally ate lunch, she still had no appetite. Nevertheless, she met Michelle in the main office and the two walked together to the cafeteria.

Eileen felt obligated to let Michelle feel useful, to let her feel as if having lunch with her and talking to her somehow helped, but it didn't. Eileen hated being on the spot now, but there was no hiding how she felt. She wondered how she'd be able to function at work if things didn't get any better.

Michelle had filled her plate with greasy chicken, fries, rolls, and a diet soda. It always occurred to Eileen that the choice of a diet soda seemed only to draw more attention to the fact that everything else on Michelle's plate was *not* for a diet. Eileen made a salad and had a bottle of water. They sat away from the crowd and in a fairly quiet area of the cafeteria. Michelle began eating while Eileen pushed and picked at her salad.

"Tell me what's happening, Eileen," said Michelle, who smothered Eileen by sitting next to her instead of across from her.

Eileen shifted her chair away and replied, "Well, I guess you could say that as bad as things had been between me and Ron, they've actually gotten worse."

"God, Eileen. I am so sorry. Is there anything I can do? Are you guys thinking of separating?"

"You know, Michelle, it's not that easy. He would *never* move out. No way. There is no way he's getting out and looking for an apartment or condo, you know. That's just not happening."

"Then why don't *you* move out?"

"My mother would just die."

"Your mother?"

"Yes. You know, the best thing that ever happened to my mother was when my father died. She was in the most awful marriage—"

"Oh God, Eileen, and you're repeating the same thing," interrupted Michelle, with a dramatic slap of the table.

"Michelle, relax!" hushed Eileen, as she reached to grab Michelle's hand. Her eyes darted about, then she leaned forward and whispered, "No, my mother's situation was worse. He drank and he was an angry drunk."

"Your father was an alcoholic?" asked Michelle, loudly, clanking her fork and knife down as if to underscore the importance of both this revelation and her presumptive need to know it. "You never told me that."

"It's not the easiest thing to just open up to people about this," said Eileen, her eyes averted.

"So wouldn't your mother be happy to see you do something about *your* marriage? She doesn't want you to stay unhappy while waiting for the day *your husband* dies, does she?"

"No, it's not that. My mother would be mortified. She'd be so embarrassed by my 'failed' marriage. *I'm* so embarrassed. You're like the only person I've told this to. I can't just leave the house and move out. God, I just can't even imagine it...I couldn't deal with that. I'd be humiliated. I'm a therapist helping other couples with their marriages and here I am running away from my problems."

"Eileen, you're not running from your problems. You're taking care of yourself. This is *not* your fault, and you shouldn't be suffering like this. You don't *have* to suffer like this. We're always the ones who have to put our interests last behind all these other concerns, like who will be embarrassed or how it will look to so and so—"

"We?" Eileen interrupted.

"Yes, 'We.' We women, I mean," explained Michelle.

"Well, Michelle, this isn't about 'we women;' it's about me and my life, and I have to deal with this as it affects *me,* not anyone else," Eileen argued, angered by Michelle's intimation that her life choices were now being evaluated within some grander context.

"I *know* it's about you, Eileen. I'm just trying to point out that you're allowing your choices in this situation to be limited by other people's concerns, instead of taking care of your needs first."

"I'm not *allowing* my choices to be limited, Mich. You don't always have choices in these situations."

"Tim thinks that—"

"Michelle! Please don't tell me you talked to your husband about my marriage."

"I don't talk to him about *your* marriage, Eileen. I was just going to tell you an observation he's made about—"

"Michelle, please! This is so embarrassing. I really don't want to hear what Tim thinks about this. I feel like I'm under a microscope already, and I don't want to think that sharing something with you is going anywhere else, including—no, *especially*—to your husband."

"Eileen, I said I did *not* share *anything* with my husband about you or your marriage," insisted Michelle. She noticed Eileen was not eating, and then she looked at her watch. "You know what? I don't think talking about this over lunch is such a good idea. You haven't touched anything, and I'm going to need to get out of here soon" she said. She smiled at Eileen, and with the tilt of her head she teetered between patronizing and sympathizing.

"I'm not even hungry right now," said Eileen.

"What time is Pagnotti coming in?"

"Oh, he's not going to be here till 2:30"

"You feel okay about that? I know the staff meeting wasn't exactly helpful the other day when you presented him."

"It'll be all right. I'll just continue setting limits as I did the other day. I won't allow him to manipulate me the way he usually does."

"What does that guy do for a living, anyway?" asked Michelle.

"He doesn't do anything. He sits around all day driving his father crazy while taking his money. What a life," said Eileen, as she began to eat now that she was off the topic of her marriage.

She was tempted to tell Michelle about Ron hitting her, but knew it was too much information to share with her. Michelle's advice would be non-stop, demanding that Eileen get out of the house, call the police, contact a support group and so on. Eileen didn't see any of that happening. What she could see happening was not talking about it, not thinking about it, not sharing it with anyone, never discussing it, just moving forward and forgetting about it. She'd always been good at forgetting bad things and this would be just another situation to forget. Even now she was beginning to feel better as she talked about the Pagnotti case.

"So basically he sits around all day taking money from his father whenever he needs it. He hates his father, and the only thing he does all week is come in to see you. Is he on disability?" asked Michelle.

"No, I shouldn't say he *always* sits around. He's had jobs in the past helping some friend with a landscaping business and things like that. The problem is his father, who provides whatever money he needs. So Brock doesn't really *have* to find a job. And when he does have a job, he doesn't have to worry about losing it because he has his father to back him up. So he can be as nasty as he wants wherever he goes or whatever job he has."

"What a slime," said Michelle, as her tongue and finger worked feverishly to extract a piece of chicken wedged between her teeth. "So what keeps his father from kicking him out?"

"It's a long story, Michelle, and you have to go see your two o'clock. Basically it's that people sometimes feel trapped in situations they can't just change like that," she said, snapping her fingers. "You can't always appreciate their situation from the outside...You know that; you're a therapist," she said, smirking as she patted Michelle on the back.

"I hear ya, Eileen," replied Michelle, rolling her eyes at Eileen's not-so-subtle implication to butt out. "So maybe you and Pagnotti's dad should get together and start your own support group for each other," she chortled.

Eileen laughed. "Yeah, we can sit around talking about what an asshole his son is."

"Well listen, I have to run. So you take care of yourself. I'll talk to you later if you have time," said Michelle, as she gathered her tray and began to leave, "are you going now?"

"I'll be up later. I think I want a frozen yogurt. This salad just isn't doing it for me."

Michelle walked out, and Eileen remained sitting and staring. She looked at the many unfamiliar faces of people scurrying about the cafeteria, as well as the many familiar ones of her colleagues. There they were—smiling, laughing, talking. Everyone else seemed animated and alive, while she felt dead. No one was going through what she was, she thought. No one.

Though her legs felt lifeless, she managed to lift herself from her chair and make her way over to the frozen yogurt. She stared at the choices, unable to make a decision while two women and a tall man stood impatiently nearby. She felt confined and paralyzed. The sounds in the cafeteria seemed to grow louder. Her chest heaved with every breath, but it felt as if she were drawing air through a straw. She could no longer think of which yogurt to choose, but instead fixated on the thought that she was about to lose control, or do something crazy.

She looked back at the three people waiting and managed a flat, apologetic smile. She was sure they could hear the *thudding* sound in her chest. She was embarrassed and scared. The thirty seconds or so she stood perplexed before the yogurt machine dragged on until her legs began to wobble and she thought she might fall over. "Are you okay?" someone asked. "I am," she replied, but instead of buying a yogurt she turned, stumbled for a moment, and finally plodded away from the yogurt machine and out a side door.

She regained control of her breath and began to calm down as she lifted her face, eyes closed, to the bright afternoon sun. After a fifteen minute walk, she returned to the mental health center and went back to her office to await her patient.

Chapter Five

P AGNOTTI HAD ARRIVED EARLY AND WAS PACING THE WAITING
room, his hands shoved deep into his pockets when Eileen
passed him on her way back from the cafeteria. "I'll be with
you in just a minute, Brock."

"Fine," Pagnotti mumbled.

When she returned to her office, Eileen sat for awhile worrying
about the "trapped feeling" happening again, as it had in the
cafeteria. It would be awful to have that happen while talking to a
patient, especially Pagnotti, she thought. How could she leave the
office if it happens again? She took three slow breaths—using the
same deep breathing she'd instructed so many of her patients to use
during their own panic attacks.

Feeling better, she went to the waiting area and walked Pagnotti
back to her office. They avoided eye contact and said nothing—the
only sound coming from the chairs as Pagnotti pulled, knocked,
and manhandled his before sitting down. Eileen slid quietly into
hers, then caught his eyes and with a quiet voice asked him how
he was doing.

"What's with the tone? What are ya takin' some training, or
did ya go to some conference on how to talk differently to nuts like
me?" asked Brock. He sat sphinx-like, staring straight ahead with
one foot resting on top of the other and arms folded across his chest.

"Brock...you're coming here to get help, right? So in my opinion that means we need to focus on helping you make changes. And to tell you the truth, I'm not quite sure where we're headed. But I'm *sure* we're not going to get anywhere by talking about what conferences or training I attend."

Eileen continued looking directly at Pagnotti, whose sideward glances gave the impression of a fish. His eye bulged out as he strained to catch a glimpse of her before quickly looking away, all the while rocking back and forth stiffly in his seat.

"And before we move into any area of your life that we're going to try to change, I need to know if you're feeling safe. Are you feeling like you want to hurt yourself?" continued Eileen, feeling more confident about this opening to the session. The anxiety she had felt earlier was gone. She sat leaning comfortably toward Pagnotti, eyebrows drawn together in a look of concern. She felt no empathy for him—any genuine concern about his well-being having died long ago—and therefore put as much energy into how she sat and how her faced looked as she put into what she said.

"Ya know what? You think that by runnin' me over to the emergency room every time I tell ya I'm thinkin' of hurtin' myself that that's gonna solve anything? Well it's not. I'm just gonna keep it to myself. It doesn't mean I feel any better. It just means I won't tell ya how I'm really feeling," said Pagnotti, in a quieter, softer tone than his revved up appearance might have suggested.

"Brock, if I don't take your words seriously, then I'm doing *you* a disservice. If you talk about wanting to hurt yourself, then I'm *obligated* to do something about that. If I ignore it, then what is *that* saying to you?"

"I don't wanna waste my time on this, okay? Can we talk about something else?" asked Pagnotti as his fidgeting gradually slowed.

Despite his wanting to change topics, Eileen pressed him, "Brock, are you having any thoughts about hurting yourself?"

He looked her in the eyes, paused and took a deep breath before blurting out, "I have a girlfriend."

"A girlfriend?" exclaimed a smiling Eileen, sinking comfortably back into her chair. "That's wonderful, Brock. How long have you known her?"

"Not long."

"What does your father think?"

"Why are you bringin' that asshole into this? How the fuck does he matter? What am I in high school?" He glared at Eileen as his voice grew louder.

"I'm sorry, Brock, really. You're right. I shouldn't have mentioned him—" she apologized.

"You're always sorry. I don't want your goddamned apologies. I don't want ya bringing that asshole into this. I'm forty-five years old, for chrissakes! Since when do ya have to get your parent's opinion about a girl when you're forty-five goddamn years old?"

"Brock, you *live* with him. He's a part of your life. I just thought that...maybe he'd be happy for you. Wouldn't that make things easier for you at home?" offered Eileen, trying to extricate herself from this dead-end by offering Pagnotti a selfish reason for sharing the good news with his father.

"I don't need to make things easier for myself or please my goddamn father! Don't you get that? I'm not doin' anything to please him," he bellowed, waving his hands and arms in the air.

Eileen always found it unsettling when others showed anger, and this was no exception. Pagnotti's jerky hand and arm movements were disturbing enough, but the way he spit his words when he became loud brought to mind her father's rage and—like an ice cube suddenly dropped down the back of her shirt—caused her to sit bolt upright, her face pallid.

She quickly shifted directions to pacify Pagnotti. "Can you tell me where you met her? Or tell me something about her?"

"It doesn't matter where I met her," he replied curtly.

"Okay, uh...well...umm...you know we've talked a lot about you getting out more and socializing. Now...well, now you have the perfect excuse. You can go out to, umm, a movie or to dinner—"

"I don't know that she's gonna wanna do that. I don't know what she wants...It's still very early."

"Well, have you asked her...you know, if she wants to go out?"

"Out? Like where?"

"Have you gone anywhere together yet?"

"Not really. We've mostly just talked."

"Okay, then maybe it would be a good idea to ask her out for a cup of coffee or for lunch as a start."

Pagnotti nodded but remained silent. Then he looked up, as if a thought suddenly occurred: "You married?" he asked.

"Am I married?" she replied with a startle. "What makes you say that?"

"Well I don't see you wearin' your ring," he said gesturing to her hand.

She looked down and immediately grasped her hand as if just discovering the ring's absence. An image of her husband shoving her flashed through her mind. She couldn't speak.

"I thought you were married. I thought I remember seein' a ring on you. Are you divorced now or somethin'?" he asked an obviously stunned Eileen. His smirk broadened as her face became flush.

Unnerved, Eileen was again put on the defensive with one of Pagnotti's classic off-topic remarks. He's so damned observant, she thought. He noticed her ring missing, which she'd taken off the night before and left in the bedroom. After the incident with Ron, and her sleeping downstairs, she had left the house quickly without putting on jewelry. Maybe she forgot it on purpose, she thought. Or maybe it was just an oversight—an interesting coincidence—but not an omen or symbol of her deteriorating marriage. In any event, she felt uncertain about answering his question. She didn't want to reward him by answering personal questions that were off topic. She fiddled with her fingers and rubbed the spot where her ring would have been while he reveled in her discomfort.

This should have been dealt with quickly and succinctly, without allowing Pagnotti to veer down irrelevant—and personal— paths. But Eileen was having trouble concentrating, and her mind was preoccupied. The image of her angry husband pushing her down hovered before her and clouded not only her thinking, but also quite literally her view of Pagnotti, who had finally stopped squirming around in his chair so he could watch Eileen fidget and twist in hers. She squeezed her eyes shut twice trying to clear them as well as her mind. He couldn't possibly know what she was going through at home—she knew this for sure—but his question about her ring gnawed at her for some reason.

She hadn't shared with Michelle that her husband hit her. She couldn't tell her mother. She felt ashamed and embarrassed by what was happening to her, and keeping this information to herself only intensified her guilt. But worse than that, she felt as if others could see through her facade. Pagnotti's questions seemed to mock her charade, she felt. It was as if he knew exactly what was going on in her personal life, and now he was tormenting her as only a mind as sick as his could.

Her throat tightened, her tongue was thick, and her stomach felt as if she were free falling in an elevator. As the room seemed to shrink around her and breathing became labored, she managed to locate a cliché among her scattered thoughts: "Brock, this isn't about me. This is about you."

"You sit here and ask people all kinds of personal questions, an' you can't even tell me if you're married or not," he persisted with his arrogance.

"Brock, I...I...I'm not sure where this is headed...or, uh, how this can help you. We...we aren't...we're not here to, um, we're not here to talk about me. This is a waste of your time," she said more assertively now, as her anxiety ebbed just a bit.

"Well, I think this whole therapy has been a waste. I'm not any better than when I started," he complained.

"I'm sorry you feel that way."

"Yeah, I'm sure you are," he said derisively.

"Maybe we should do something about that."

"Well, that's what ya get paid for, isn't it? And I don't see ya earning yer money. I come here every week and I'm as miserable as ever. I can't stand my life. My father pisses me off—"

"Let's do something about that," she interrupted, leaping at the reference to his father.

"About what?"

"About your father pissing you off."

"I don't wanna talk about my goddamn father," he said, his voice rising again.

"It's not just your father who upsets you, Brock. It's me too. And, and, and it's people you've worked for. And it's salespeople and the secretaries, and the security people downstairs—"

"So now I'm totally fucked up, is that it?"

"I didn't say that, Brock. You have problems with your anger. And...and...I mean, you have a right to feel like that, but at some point you have to learn to let go of it. It holds you back and makes you miserable. It gets you into trouble—"

"I have to let go of it? I FUCKIN' have to let go of it!" He ran one hand nervously through his hair and rubbed his thigh vigorously with the other as if soothing a sore muscle. He made no eye contact and his voice raged. It was as if he were in his own world now. "What about my fuckin' mother? She just fuckin' kills herself. She didn't give a goddamn about me, did she?

"Brock—"

"Did she? She didn't have to let go of anything. Why am I the only goddamned one who has to 'let go of it,'" he said, mocking her words with an exaggerated, high-pitched squeal.

"Brock—"

"MY FATHER DOESN'T HAVE TO LET GO OF ANYTHING! I'M THE ONE. I'M THE ONE WHO HAS TO CHANGE," he shouted, waving his hand in the air. *"I'm* the one who has to clean up the mess that those assholes left!"

His hand came down, pounding the desk—harder and harder, over and over and over again his fist struck. She'd seen him angry before, but not like this; he was out of control. She sat motionless, holding her breath and unable to speak as he flailed away.

Then he stopped almost as abruptly as he'd begun. He covered his face with his hands and leaned forward with his elbows on his knees. After several silent minutes, he sat up and stared at her through glassy eyes.

"Brock, are you okay?" she uttered through a dry, brittle voice.

"I'm sorry I did that," he said in a monotone, his complexion whitish as the blood that filled his face during the tirade seemed suddenly to drain away. He looked as though he were going to be sick.

With Pagnotti's rage over, Eileen was able to assume her supportive front. She spoke about the small accomplishments he'd made in the past and expressed sympathy as best she could; but she struggled as he seemed in another world, his eyes distant, as if without his fury he was empty.

They finished the session and Pagnotti left the office with another appointment scheduled for next week. Eileen gathered her belongings and went to Dr. Thomas to ask if she could leave early.

"I'm not feeling well. Can you have someone cancel the rest of my patients. I think it's only like two more. The last one on my schedule already canceled. I really need to get home."

"Go, go, go. Don't worry about anything. We'll take care of it. Go home and get some rest," replied Dr. Thomas, placing her hand on Eileen's back and gently pushing her out.

"Thanks, Diane, I really appreciate it." said Eileen, and she turned and walked out.

Moments later, Michelle walked into the office and overheard Dr. Thomas telling the secretaries to cancel Eileen's patients.

"Did Eileen go home early?" asked Michelle.

"Yes, she looked awful," answered Dr. Thomas.

"Oh!" Michelle exclaimed, and the room became silent.

"Is everything all right?" Dr. Thomas asked Michelle.

"I don't know. I mean, she seemed okay at lunch. I think she just needs some time away from her patients, you know? I'm sure she'll be okay."

"Are you sure, Michelle?" asked Dr. Thomas.

"No, really...I...I...I was just surprised, that's all. You know, she's...she's having a hard time."

"A hard time?"

"You know, she's got some tough patients. I just think she needs some time off."

"Tough patients?"

"Yeah, tough patients. You know, we all need some time off now and then. Some of these patients can really get to you."

"Okay, well...I appreciate that. Thank you, Michelle," Dr. Thomas said, still puzzled.

Michelle walked out, and the secretaries looked at Dr. Thomas, who looked back at the door Michelle had just left through.

"Strange," Dr. Thomas muttered, "very strange."

Exhausted, Eileen fell asleep on the loveseat for several hours as soon as she arrived home. Ron was still out when she woke up at 8:30 that night. She sat up slowly, stretched her arms over her head and then moved her left arm in a circular motion, testing its range and looking for pain. She found none.

She sat for awhile longer, feeling alone and sorry for herself. Her marriage was crumbling; her work was suffering; the panic attacks were happening more often. She paced around the house and finally her restlessness and anxiety led her to the computer, where she logged on to check her email and see if her "friend" was online. How pathetic, she thought, having to chat with an anonymous stranger to provide what her real life couldn't.

But her self-pity vanished with a few keystrokes. No more than a minute after logging on, Sweetdude35 sent Eileen a message: "Hey Cheeryl, I've been waiting for you."

She smiled broadly at his words. He was so carefree and playful, she thought. He was a stranger, and he was just words on the screen, but his presence was palpable and his *real*ness filled a void. She liked sitting alone before the computer with nothing but its humming and the tapping of the keys, and she enjoyed the one-to-one connection with a stranger; *this* stranger who seemed to care, who reached out to her, who seemed sweet and sincere. She wasted no time responding, telling him what she was unable to share with anyone in person.

"My husband hurt me," she said, although the words alone stood bare, stripped of her emotional pain. Her chat buddy couldn't see her—he couldn't see her tears, her lower lip quivering, her fingers trembling. He couldn't know about the knot in her stomach.

"Hurt you? What do you mean hurt you?" asked Sweetdude35, not yet sensing the gravity of what she was saying.

"He pushed me. Hard. I fell over."

"OH MY GOD! HE HURT YOU PHYSICALLY?" replied Sweetdude35.

"Yes, he hurt me physically. I don't know what to do."

"That fucker has no right to lay a hand on you. When did this happen?"

"Last night."

"Where is he now?"

"I don't know. I slept downstairs last night and he left early in the morning before I got up. He's still not home now."

"Are you going to stay there?"

"Where else would I stay?"

"Can I call you?"

Eileen paused, not so much shocked by his offer, but intrigued. She was startled by her reaction; she didn't find his request outrageous, as she might have in the beginning.

She finally replied, "I don't feel comfortable just giving out my number to you," not completely ruling it out, but rather inviting him to figure out how it could be done.

"Well, I'd be O.K. about you calling me. Then you wouldn't be giving out your number," he suggested.

She considered this, but thought about caller ID and how he could easily get her number even if she called him. Her heart was racing now with both fear and excitement.

"You could still use star sixty-nine or have caller ID. How do I know you won't call my house at some other time?" she asked.

She offered these arguments, which Sweetdude35—like her, handicapped by the lack of tone, volume, inflections, facial expression and the like—interpreted as firm opposition. But Eileen's concerns were neither excuses (like "I'm busy Saturday night") nor firm; rather, she was considering various pitfalls from a perspective of cautious willingness. She didn't fully oppose his idea; she was simply hoping Sweetdude35 could come up with a reasonably safe way to make this happen. She longed to talk to someone who would listen to her and care about her. All she needed was for him to convince her that their privacy could be protected, for she was now already over the line toward accepting his offer. But the complexity of what was happening between them was lost in the plainness of their exchanges appearing as just text on the computer screen.

"I understand you don't feel safe. It's not a big deal. We don't have to talk on the phone," he relented rather easily.

She paused to think. A million ideas swirled in her mind.

"Are you mad at me?" he interrupted her unresponsiveness.

"No," she replied immediately. "I didn't say I didn't want to talk. I'm thinking about this. I just want to be careful. Can we come back to this another time? Let me have more time to think."

"Tell me what happened," he said.

"I wanted to talk to him last night because I had things on my mind. He was just sitting in front of the T.V. I went to turn it off, and he stood up and pushed me. He pushed me hard enough that I fell backwards."

"Oh my god! Are you afraid to be home with him?"

"I don't know. I feel miserable. Mostly I feel embarrassed. I feel trapped. I hate how this feels."

"God, I am so sorry to hear this. This is unbelievable. I wish I could be there for you."

"Thank you. In a way, you are. I haven't told this to anyone. You're the first person."

"You need to do something about this. Has he done this kind of thing before?" asked Sweetdude35.

"No, thank God, no. This is a first, but I have such a hard time with other people's anger. It scares me. My father used to be like that. He'd get so angry and raise his voice that he'd scare the hell out of all of us. I don't want to be in the kind of situation my mother was in," she continued, greatly relieved she could let her thoughts and feelings flow freely to Sweetdude35.

It almost didn't matter that anyone else was on the other end receiving this. It felt good to express it. There was, however, an undeniable connection—a bonding—that she felt toward Sweetdude35, this anonymous listener, simply because he was *there*. And he listened well, as well as one can listen online. He let her vent and his replies were supportive, not judgmental.

"Do you have family?" he asked.

"I have a sister and my mother. They both live nearby. My father died awhile ago."

"Why don't you go stay with your sister or mother," he suggested.

"I can't impose on my sister."

"And your mother?"

"I can't"

"Why?" he pressed her. "Is she sick?"

"No. She's fine. But I'd have to explain what happened, and she would just be so judgmental."

"My dad can be judgmental too, so I definitely know how that feels. But it's important for you to have some kind of support right now."

"I know. I know." She was struck by his insight. It was as if she were talking to one of her colleagues, she marveled.

"Besides, who knows what happens next," he said. "A guy with that kind of anger can really hurt you. You don't know what he's going to do."

"You are so sweet to me, and you do make a lot of sense. Maybe I will see my mother. I don't even know where my husband is or when he's coming home."

"Do you think he's coming home at all?" he asked.

"He's never just *not* come home. Maybe he's hoping I'll be asleep when he comes home, and that way he can avoid talking to me."

"Maybe when he comes home he ought to find you gone. Then he'll get the message that he can't treat you this way."

"Well I can't go to my mother's tonight because it's too late. Maybe I'll call in sick tomorrow and go visit her for the day."

They continued chatting awhile longer. His reasoning finally convinced her to take care of herself by getting some support from someone. She felt so great talking to him; she was beginning to believe she could tell him anything. She hadn't felt this good in days, so she decided to reveal something she had backed away from earlier.

"I have a secret to tell you," she said teasingly.

"A secret, eh," he replied.

"Yep."

And she paused.

He waited.

"Well????" he asked, conveying his impatience with multiple question marks.

"Remember you told me you're from New Jersey?"

"NO WAY!" he replied, immediately and correctly assuming what she meant by her question.

"What do you mean NO WAY? No way, what? You don't even know what I'm going to tell you," she teased, smiling broadly as her nails clicked and tapped excitedly across the keyboard.

"Are you in New Jersey? Tell me if you are! Where in New Jersey?"

"Calm down. Don't get carried away. For all I know you're in Cape May or Atlantic City."

There was a pause, then, "What a bummer. Don't tell me you're from way down south Jersey, are you?"

"Why? Are you thinking of visiting me?" she continued teasing, emboldened by the comfort she felt with him, and by the concern, warmth, and genuine excitement he conveyed to her.

"Oh my God! Tell me you're kidding," he asked in disbelief.

"Kidding about what?" she asked, gently biting her lower lip as she smiled.

She continued her flirting, playfully alternating provocative statements with innocence and naiveté.

"Come on," he said, "at least tell me what county you're in."

"I'm in Bergen County," she answered without hesitation. But after a long pause there was still no response from him. "Hello? You still there?" she typed again and again.

The delay continued through several minutes. Eileen was puzzled, but remained online waiting for a reply. Maybe the computer server was jammed with too much traffic tonight, she thought. She sat back and pulled out a cigarette, lighting it while keeping one eye on the screen in order to catch his reappearance as soon as it happened. Still waiting, she walked into the kitchen and poured herself a glass of white wine, then returned to the computer. "You there?" she typed, but still no reply.

Back in Sweetdude35's bedroom, where he'd just been typing away on the computer, there was a weak knock on the door, which had distracted him from his chat. He turned away from the computer screen and now stood facing the door, as his father entered the room without an invitation.

"What the FUCK are you doin' in here?" bellowed Sweetdude35, his hands clenched in fists while glaring at his father.

"I was about to—" his father began matter-of-factly, but he was cut off by his son.

"I DON'T CARE WHAT YOU'RE ABOUT TO DO! WHO THE HELL ARE YOU TO BARGE INTO MY ROOM WHEN I'M WORKING!" he roared, charging at his father until their noses were no more than an inch or two apart.

"What the hell is wrong with you?" his father reacted, standing up to his son with a stern, coarse voice, "You're not some guest in a hotel here. You're my son and I wanted to ask you a question," he said indignantly, his lips pressed firmly together in a protruding frown while staring his son directly in the eyes.

Eileen was finishing her smoke, still curious where her partner had gone. She tried again to summon his presence on the screen, "Hello???? Are you there? What happened?" No reply as, unbeknownst to her, the clash between Sweetdude35 and his father was escalating. She refilled her glass with more wine.

"You're a lazy no good bum and you should be ashamed of yourself, talking to your father like this. You don't have any respect for anything or anyone," his father yelled.

"Why don't ya go back to bed, ya old man. You should be dead, ya miserable waste of a life. You're wasting space, now get the hell out of my room!" shouted Sweetdude35. Then he lunged toward his father shoving him as forcefully as he could and knocking him back over the threshold and down a short staircase. His head banged hard against the wall where the staircase began a right angle turn toward the living room.

Sitting slumped over and motionless for awhile, his father reached up to feel the blood oozing from the side of his head. "Get me to a doctor, you son of a bitch" he said. "Look what you've done to me. Look at this, you goddamned son of a bitch!"

Chapter Six

ILEEN GAVE UP AFTER TRYING SEVERAL MORE TIMES TO ATTRACT Sweetdude35's attention. She shut down the computer, walked upstairs to bed, and was asleep for three hours when the phone startled her. Confused and a little dizzy after snapping upright in bed, she hesitated, staring at the phone wondering if it had rung or if she had dreamed it. It rang again, raising goose bumps down her back and along her shoulders and arms. She pulled the covers up to warm herself and to stop the trembling. Before it rang a third time, she realized Ron was still out. She quickly reached over and grabbed the phone before the machine picked up.

"Hello?"

"Mrs. Duet?" said a woman's voice on the other end.

"Yes?" Eileen replied, her midsection quivering in response to the woman's deep and formal tone.

"I'm calling from Ridge Memorial Hospital. Your husband has been in a car accident, and he's in critical condition. We've been trying to reach you but your—"

"What did you say? Oh my god! Did I hear you right? Where is he?"

"Mrs. Duet?"

"Is he alive?"

"Mrs. Duet, if—"

"Please tell me what's going on here!" Eileen shouted.

"Mrs. Duet, I understand this is upsetting and may be too much to handle right now, so if you can give me another family member's phone number, we'll call them to come pick you up? Your line has been busy and we tried to reach you earlier. Your husband's alive but he's in critical condition. You need to get here now," said the woman, continuing in her serious but matter-of-fact tone.

"WHY DIDN'T YOU CALL ME? IS HE GOING TO BE OKAY?" Eileen shrieked at the woman.

"Mrs. Duet, your husband is in critical condition. As I said, I suggest you come now. Can we contact another family member?" the woman asked again.

But there was silence as the woman's words, 'your husband is in critical condition,' seized hold of Eileen's mind and echoed over and over again.

"Mrs. Duet? Are you there Mrs. Duet?"

"Yes. I'm sorry. I...uh...I...I'm here...I'm okay. I will be there. I'm only twenty minutes from there. I'll come right now."

"Mrs. Duet, please let me see if I can contact a family member for you. Is there—"

"NO! I mean, no thank you. That won't be necessary, really. I can make it there."

"Are you sure?"

"Yes, really. Yes, I appreciate what you're saying, but please, let me just get myself dressed, and I'll be there as soon as I can."

She hung up the phone after finally convincing the stubborn woman she would be capable of driving herself to the hospital. Still in shock, she sat for a moment on the end of the bed—catastrophic thoughts melding with horrifying images as her head began to throb. Then she jumped up, struggled briefly to open her bottom drawer and frantically pulled out a pair of sweats. She felt detached from her body, as if she were observing herself from a distance going through the motions. She finished dressing, ran down the stairs, grabbed her keys and was out the door, wondering how she was directing her legs when she couldn't feel them moving.

Questions swirled through her head: *What was he doing? Where had he been all day and night? Was he drinking? Was this my fault? Did I get him so upset that he couldn't think straight? I can't believe I was on the goddamn computer and they were trying to get through to me. I can't believe this!*

"I'm an idiot! It's all my fault!" she yelled out loud as she banged her hands on the steering wheel.

She was both surprised and angry at the number of cars on the road at this time of night, or rather at this early hour in the morning. Where in the world are people going at this hour, she thought. It took half an hour to get to Ridge Memorial. It was drizzling outside and the wipers seemed to smear the raindrops across the windshield. She arrived at the hospital and pulled into the large semi-circle driveway that brought her to the emergency room entrance. She left her car there—she was three steps away when she had to go back and close the car door she'd left open—and raced into the hospital.

Breathless, she stopped at the reception area where she loudly and frantically demanded to a heavy-set, red-haired woman, "Where is my husband? Where can I see him?"

"Just a second ma'am. What's your husband's name?" asked the woman politely.

"His name is Ron Duet. Ron Duet, please! He was in a car accident! Please I need to see him!"

"Ah, the motor vehicle accident. Come with me, Mrs. Duet." She led Eileen through a maze of doors and corridors where they were greeted by a rush of sights and sounds. Nurses squeaked around the floors, lights glared, patients in wheelchairs sat in the hallways hooked up to monitoring machines, a person moaned for help. Metal and lights were everywhere. They finally arrived in a small waiting area where the woman placed one hand on Eileen's shoulder and motioned with the other, "why don't you have a seat here," she said.

"Where is he? When can I see him?" she cried.

"Dr. Stanton will be right with you. Would you like a cup of coffee? Or some juice?" asked the woman.

"No, nothing. Thanks. What is his name? Stanson?"

"It's Stanton. Dr. Stanton. He'll be here shortly." The woman turned and walked away.

The wait seemed endless, but was more like two or three minutes when Eileen spotted a black, thin, balding man with a goatee approaching her.

"Dr. Stanton? Are you Dr. Stanton?" asked Eileen.

"Mrs. Duet?" he asked softly.

"Yes, I'm his wife. Are you Dr. Stanton? Is my husband going to be all right?"

"Yes, I'm Dr. Stanton. Please, have a seat." He placed one hand gently over hers and supported her elbow with the other as he guided her to a seat.

He looked her in the eyes, took a deep breath and bit his lip before beginning, "Your husband has been in a terrible accident; just awful. He suffered massive chest trauma and head injuries. You need to know that his chances...well...his chances are looking pretty poor at this point."

Tears streamed down Eileen's face and she started to shake. "No! No! No!" she cried as she banged both fists against Dr. Stanton's chest. Dr. Stanton held her arms by the wrists while she writhed weakly before giving up and sinking into his comforting embrace.

They sat together for five minutes without saying anything. Finally, Eileen sat up and asked, "Can I see him?"

"Yes, of course you can see him," he answered immediately. "He can't respond to you, but it wouldn't hurt for him to hear your voice."

Eileen put her hands to her face, bent forward toward her knees and sobbed quietly. Dr. Stanton placed his hand on her back and continued, "Even if he does regain consciousness, he's not going to be himself. We're unsure right now how much he'll be able to say or do."

He paused as she continued to sob.

"I'm very sorry, Mrs. Duet," he offered, his eyes moist and his voice betraying a hint of emotion. He put his arm on her shoulder as she cried into her hands.

Dr. Stanton led Eileen through more corridors and up an elevator to the room where Ron lay, wires sprouting from him and a tube inserted into his mouth. The room had a sterile scent, and the lights, beeping, and humming quickly overloaded Eileen's senses. She felt a panic attack building inside her and so she stopped abruptly, placing one hand on the wall and one across her chest.

"Are you okay? Do you want me to get a chair?" asked Dr. Stanton.

"No, no. I'll be all right. I'm...I...I just need to...get my breath," she replied, sucking in a deep breath, holding it and then slowly and deliberately whistling it out like an inflatable raft losing air. The anxiety subsided quickly, but she stood in the threshold while Dr. Stanton waited for her next move.

She took several steps, then seemed to hurtle toward the bed and began to cry, tears falling onto Ron, who lay connected to a respirator. The left side of his head was heavily bandaged. "NO!" and "Oh my God! Why did this have to happen? Why? It's all my fault!" she moaned repeatedly as Dr. Stanton did his best to console her.

Eileen stayed with her husband over the next twelve hours as his battle to survive lost ground precipitously. During that time, her mother, Kelly, and Michelle visited to offer support. Ron Duet finally died a little over twenty-four hours after the car accident. Eileen moved through the next several days as if in a trance. Funeral arrangements were made by her sister and mother, who carried on in a very business-like manner.

She spent much of the time blaming herself for Ron's death. She felt she had been unusually provocative the night before his death, that she had placed too much pressure on him when he was already dealing with stress at work, and that if she had just kept quiet none of this would have happened.

Her sister and Michelle alternately consoled her with kind words and admonished her for taking responsibility for the accident. After two weeks leave from work and smothered by the support of Kelly and Michelle, Eileen uncharacteristically asserted her right to privacy and cut herself off from everyone. She returned to work a week later, but when she came home afterwards she wanted to be alone so she could begin the difficult process of sorting through Ron's belongings. She said little if anything to colleagues at work about how she felt, often behaving as if nothing in her life had changed as she went about her business seeing patients and completing her paperwork. She asked that her patients simply be told that she was off for personal reasons.

Although she kept to herself at work and had shunned any further support from Kelly and Michelle, she continued every night before bed to log onto the computer and chat with her friend Sweetdude35, to whom she laid bare all her confused thoughts and ambivalent feelings. She confided in him about her childhood and her alcoholic father. She told him more about her relationship to Ron and how it had turned sour. She blamed herself for what happened, and without debating the merits of her irrational self-thrashing, Sweetdude35 patiently and very judiciously challenged her thinking.

She came to crave his presence online, his insight, his support, and his good sense of humor. She never mentioned—and to be sure, it may simply have escaped her—that a considerable contributor to her increasing candor online was her habit of drinking wine while chatting. Sweetdude35 soon became associated with a light buzz, strong emotions, and a catharsis of sorts.

She thought many times during their conversations that this must be what therapy feels like for her patients, and she'd tell him what a wonderful therapist he'd make—a comment to which he usually responded by asking "is that a compliment or a put-down?" Sweetdude35 avoided talking about himself. He asked her questions and provided supportive words. He occasionally asked about calling her on the phone, but she was still rather wary about taking that step.

During one online chat session, Eileen was expressing how depressed she had been and what a difficult time she was having. Sweetdude35 wisely encouraged her to procure some support from her mother. Her sister had been uncharacteristically distant since Ron's death, and Michelle had been characteristically overbearing with her opinions. Although Eileen's mother was by nature judgmental and critical, she was, after all, her mother.

"You may be surprised by her. Maybe you just need to give her a chance," Sweetdude35 speculated.

"It's so difficult. You have to actually see her face to know what I'm talking about. If you just hear what she says, you'd never get the whole picture. It's the smirk or the raised eyebrow, or the way she shakes her head. She can be so condescending. It drives me nuts," Eileen carried on.

"You know what? I wish I had a mother, even if it was to disagree with. You don't know how lucky you are to have her around. Why don't you stay with her for awhile or invite her to stay with you. Let her take care of you for awhile. You need it. You definitely need it."

"Sweetdude35, you are soooooo good to me. Why?"

"Why? Because I care about you. I really do."

"I know you do. And you know what, you are so right about getting help. I tell that to people all the time. I should listen to my own recommendations, don't you think?" she said.

"I'd actually prefer if you have her come over to *your* house, so that way we can keep chatting at night. Otherwise, I'm gonna miss you!"

She had finished three-quarters of a bottle of wine and was feeling relaxed and loose when she offered, "you know, maybe we should get together for a cup of coffee sometime—somewhere in public where we'll both feel safe. We could meet in public and still keep our private lives anonymous till we feel completely safe."

She smiled in anticipation of his reaction. She knew that after her unyielding stance against phone contact between them, her unexpected offering of an actual get-together would shock him.

She was giddy now; sitting back, she reached for a cigarette while waiting for his reply. She adored his attention and his support, but she also delighted in the sense of control she felt when she teased him. She knew she could run his feelings in circles in a way she had never done in a real life relationship. More and more she came to believe that Sweetdude35 brought out the *real* Eileen, the Eileen that had been suppressed for so long—by her abusive father, by her quick-tempered husband, and even by her cold mother. With Sweetdude35 she could be herself and she liked who she was.

He finally replied, "Yeah, right. I can't call you on the phone, but now you're going to meet me? You're a real good tease, aren't you?"

"I knew you were going to say that. I'm not teasing though."

"Come on, don't do this to me!!"

"What am I doing? I'm willing to have a cup of coffee with you. I'm not teasing. I'm not talking about right this minute, but we will meet—I promise you," she declared.

"Well, I'll believe it when I see it, O.K.?"

"Wow, I thought you'd be going nuts right now. You don't really believe me, do you?"

"I AM going nuts, you just can't see me. But I definitely don't want you to hurt me by disappointing me. That would be very bad," he said.

How odd, she thought. *'That would be very bad.'* It almost seemed menacing, but it was impossible to judge these things when you're reading only the words and can't see the person's face.

She switched topics as she brought their chat to a close. "I'm going to call my mother in just a minute and see if I can arrange to stay with her. So if you don't see me on here in the next couple of days you'll know where I am, right?"

"Take care of yourself, O.K.? I'm going to miss you."

"Oh, I'm sure you'll be on here chatting with some other woman, cheating on me, right? Hahaha," she teased.

"Nahhhh, you're the only one for me. I'll keep checking for you. Take care of yourself and get some sleep and LET YOUR MOM HELP YOU."

"I will! I will!"

"And just ignore what she does. Don't read into her mannerisms or her face, O.K.?" Sweetdude35 cautioned her.

"I swear, if you were a therapist I'd owe you like hundreds of dollars. Do you realize that?" she replied.

"Ah, I'm just giving you my two cents. Now go take care of yourself."

"Thanks, Sweetdude35! You're a sweetheart!"

"You too. Talk to you soon."

They exchanged goodbyes and then logged off. Her concerns about staying with her mother were erased by the excitement she felt knowing she would soon take that step (finally) to meet this stranger—this stranger who knew her as no one else did, she thought. It was thrilling. It seemed so right...and yet it would be so wrong.

Chapter Seven

ILEEN'S MOTHER, HELEN KESWICK, WAS IN HER EARLY SEVENTIES, a diminutive woman whose skin still clung tightly to her bony figure. She let her close-cropped hair remain gray and never wore makeup. ("You shouldn't dirty up your skin with that poison!") Her glasses were large and round with thick lenses that made her eyes bulge, so she always looked alarmed or frightened. She lived alone—with the exception of two cats—about an hour south of Eileen, in a one bedroom condominium. Every morning at six-thirty she'd wake up and walk three blocks to a bagel shop for a newspaper, a cup of coffee, and a toasted poppy seed bagel with nothing on it. ("They don't have the right kind of butter.") She'd return home to eat about half the bagel, which she neatly and carefully dunked in her coffee. She'd then drink no more than four or five sips of coffee while reading the obituaries. She never read any other section. After finishing the obituary section, she'd take the nearly unread paper—neatly folded—to her pile of recycled papers, untie the string that held them together and stack the fresh paper on top, re-tying the string in a knot. There were always ten papers to a bundle and four bundles to a recycling bin. She liked things orderly.

In her younger days, before being widowed, Mrs. Keswick kept her opinions to herself. She accepted her role as mother and wife and caretaker, and never questioned her husband or asked for any change in the increasingly brutal treatment he dished out to her. After her husband's death, she experienced a rebirth of sorts. There was no longer any gray area or in-between for Mrs. Keswick; everything was black or white. She knew right from wrong and never missed an opportunity to tell you how things ought to be. It seemed the only ones who could tolerate her opinions were the cats, and that was only because they had no choice.

Eileen, in an effort to keep peace with her mother, rarely spoke back or questioned her opinions. This often resulted in one-sided conversations, but she desperately wanted to make the relationship work, and so she kept coming back time and time again only to be hurt by her mother's subtle yet ceaseless opinions and put-downs. It was her mother's way or the wrong way.

Eileen understood all this, and yet she believed her tragedy now presented an opportunity to bring the two of them together. She would seek solace from her mother, allowing her the opportunity to share whatever wisdom or compassion she could muster in the wake of Ron's death. Having been through it herself, Mrs. Keswick would surely know what her daughter *should* and *should not* be doing to grieve properly. Her mother knew the right way to do everything. So the bottom line here, Eileen thought, is that I'm visiting my mother not for myself but for *her*—to give *her* the chance to feel good about *herself.* Uggghh...it was sickening, she thought, but true.

Eileen threw a change of clothes and her toiletries into a backpack and headed to her mother's. She arrived early Friday evening expecting to stay till late Sunday. Her mother, standing just outside her condo as Eileen pulled into a parking space in front, walked slowly down the steps to greet her daughter.

"I thought you were getting here early," her mother began.

"Well, I had to work, but I did leave a little early. This is a lot earlier than I would have gotten here," replied Eileen, opening the passenger door to pull out her backpack.

"Don't you have a regular suitcase? You stuffed everything into that knapsack, and I'll bet everything's wrinkled now," said her mother.

"Oh, Mom."

"What 'Oh Mom'?"

"I'm only staying a couple of nights, mother. Besides, this is a lot easier to carry," said Eileen, already sensing the usual tension as her mother jumped right in with her criticisms. They walked together up the steps and inside the condo.

"Can you take your shoes off please, honey, I've just cleaned the floors. Thank you!" her mother called back as she carried Eileen's knapsack to the living room.

"Yes, mother," she answered, slipping off her shoes. Then she walked into the kitchen, filled the kettle with water and placed it on the stove to make tea.

"I thought we were going to have dinner. Don't tell me you've eaten already," said her mother, entering the kitchen.

"Of course I haven't eaten. I want to have dinner; I just wanted a cup of tea to warm up a bit."

Her mother placed both hands on her hips, shook her head side to side slowly and deliberately, then walked over to the stove and turned the burner off.

"I was going to make a pot of coffee after dinner. Can't you have coffee after dinner?" she griped. "Let's just get dinner prepared, and then we'll have coffee. You always like to do things backwards, don't you Eileen?"

Two days like this was quickly looking like an insurmountable forty-eight hours, Eileen feared. It turned out, however, that her mother softened a bit as they prepared dinner together. They ate in the kitchen and afterwards—just as it should be, according to her mother—they drank coffee. They talked about Eileen's work, about the neighbors, about Atlantic City, and about the cats. The conversation then happened upon Eileen's sister.

"Have you talked to Kelly lately?" asked Eileen, as she poured a second cup of coffee.

"I can't believe that that girl is related to you. I've never seen a more selfish person."

"Wow, is that a compliment for me? I'm not as selfish as my sister," Eileen chuckled.

"Eileen, I always tell you how giving you are. Come on, don't talk to your mother like that."

"I'm kidding, ma. What happened now? What is she up to?"

"It's no specific thing now. It's just that she's constantly dumping those kids off here, like I'm her permanent babysitter. And then, God forbid if I need her to run an errand for me, she's too busy. She just doesn't think of other people, Eileen. Oh, you know how she is," she complained, as she chewed on Ritz crackers she was dunking into her coffee.

She continued complaining as the topic of Kelly seemed to enliven her. At least it kept her from criticizing me, Eileen thought. But then her mother veered into a more sensitive area.

"And you tell me why a sister spends so much time with her sister's husband. I'm not looking to upset you, or anything. But tell me honestly, Eileen, didn't that bother you?"

Eileen froze at once, her coffee cup perched on her lips. Her mother was in rare form, but it was this last comment that particularly stung. Although Eileen had occasionally wondered about the amount of time Kelly and Ron spent together, it really wasn't *that* much, she felt (or more likely convinced herself). And she certainly never shared any concerns with her mother.

She placed her cup down, scrunched her face up in the most exaggerated look of befuddlement and asked, "What in the world are you talking about?"

"Oh stop, Eileen. We don't need to play these games anymore."

"Ma, they knew each other as long as Ron and I knew each other. They were friends. It really wasn't a big deal."

"It is a big deal. To a mother, it's a big deal! You know I never said anything; but it was just downright selfish. She thinks only of herself and *her* needs—" her mother continued, slamming her hand to the table for emphasis.

"What? Mom, have you...what are you talking about?" Eileen broke her off, outraged by her mother's sudden outburst. *What needs was she talking about? Needs that Ron was fulfilling? What does any of this have to do with Ron and Kelly,* she wondered.

"I'm talking about their relationship, Eileen. I know you and Ron were having problems—"

"Mother!" Eileen interrupted again, "our problems had nothing to do with Kelly."

"I'm not saying the problems had something to do with Kelly. But whatever the problems were between the two of you—and I don't know what those problems were; it's none of my business, I know—but when a man is unhappy at home, you know, well, he'll look elsewhere," her mother went on, the corner of her mouth pulled to the side as she looked skeptically at Eileen's denials.

"Mother! What are you saying?" she cried. "Are you kidding? Please tell me you're kidding!"

"Oh, Eileen, stop being so Goddamned naïve."

Eileen jumped up and took several steps back as if her mother had suddenly burst into flames.

"Mother! This is really, really upsetting me. I really don't appreciate what you're implying," she asserted.

She was used to criticism, but Eileen was completely unprepared for what her mother was saying. This was not a topic that had *ever* come up between them. For some reason, instead of seeing this as a time to support her grieving daughter, Mrs. Keswick elected to use her daughter's loss as a chance to share whatever rumors or assumptions she held, without concern for the implications this had for either of her daughters. She just figured now would be as good a time as any to express her opinions, as if Ron's not being there meant it was okay to make accusations about him.

"Just sit down now, Eileen. Stop getting so hysterical," her mother replied. "Here, I'll get you some more coffee. Now just calm down." Appearing oblivious to her daughter's reaction, Mrs. Keswick went to the stove with Eileen's cup to pour some more coffee.

"Forget the coffee, mom. Let's just forget this. I don't need this right now. I don't need to be made upset like this," said Eileen, pushing her chair in and storming out of the kitchen.

Her mother called out, "Eileen? Eileen? Where are you going? Now just stop this. Just stop this right now!"

But Eileen had already gathered her knapsack and keys and was headed out when she stopped in the hallway before the door. Her mother stood defiantly, arms folded across her chest.

"I'm sorry for yelling," Eileen apologized. "Let's just end this now before it goes any further. Thank you for the dinner. Let's just leave this as a nice dinner, and I appreciate that you went out of your way to have me here, but I cannot stay, okay? I think it's best for both of us."

"Oh Eileen, you're being ridiculous. You're too sensitive. You take everything the wrong way. I wasn't saying anything about *you*—"

"Please mother, let's end it here, *please?*"

"But Eileen."

"No!" said Eileen. They argued further, Mrs. Keswick pleading for her daughter to stay overnight, but Eileen adamant she could not last even one night. Finally, Eileen silenced her mother by leaning forward and kissing her on the cheek and ignoring her pleas. She turned and walked out the door.

Amazing, she thought driving home that night, that her mother could still aggravate and annoy her as no one else could. *I don't hate her, but honestly, I don't like her.* She began to cry as she thought about how much she longed for the kind of mother she could turn to at a time like this.

Her feelings were mixed between anger (at her mother) and a profound sense of loss. It was not only that her husband was gone and she now was pulling into an empty house; she also had no family or friends to turn to. Her sister was behaving in a peculiar way, and despite how angry Eileen had become over her mother's insinuations, she *was* bothered by the close relationship that had existed between her husband and sister. They *did* spend too much time together when you really thought about it. Moreover, she knew that whatever business went on between her and Ron, Kelly always knew the details; nothing could be kept secret from her. And despite Kelly's frequent expressions of sympathy and concern for her sister's marital difficulties, the gestures always seemed hollow—like an actor simply speaking the lines and going through the motions.

Eileen spoke to no one at work about her problems, other than Michelle. Michelle, however, was unbearable. Instead of supporting Eileen emotionally, she was intrusive and increasingly judgmental. The more suggestions she made about how Eileen *must* be feeling or what she *must* be thinking, the more Eileen pulled back. So it was with no hesitation that immediately upon returning home, Eileen headed straight to the computer, eager to dump her feelings on her anonymous online buddy. He had become, she believed, the only one to whom she could truly relate. He offered support, insight, and sound judgment— notwithstanding his bad idea about visiting her mother, she thought, now smiling to herself.

While the computer buzzed and whirred and beeped its way on, Eileen went to the kitchen for a bottle of white wine and an ashtray. She slipped her shoes off, walked back to the study and sat down at the computer. She pointed and clicked on the browser's icon to log on. When she was connected, she clicked on her chat program's icon and logged on to that. She typed a search for Sweetdude35's name, and then immediately slumped back down in her chair in disappointment when the search indicated he was offline. She lit a cigarette and poured a second glass of wine to relax as she waited in a sulk.

No more than three or four minutes had passed when a window opened on her screen with text written in bold and all caps, **"WHAT ARE YOU DOING BACK SO SOON? WHAT HAPPENED?"** It was Sweetdude35.

"My God, you have no idea how happy I am to see you. I just got on and looked for you but you weren't here. You must have just logged on. How did you find me so quickly?" she asked, her fingers tapping away at the keyboard as fast as her thoughts raced.

"I have you on my permanent notification list. As soon as I log on, if you're on, it tells me. But tell me what happened??? Why are you back? I thought you were staying till Sunday night?" he asked.

"I know, I know. I wasn't supposed to be back this early, but as soon as I got there I was ready to leave! This has been an awful day. I just can't take more than a few hours with that woman. You have no idea what she's like."

"Yes I do. I think my father must be related to your mother hahaha," he joked.

"Well, I don't think anyone can match my mother," replied Eileen. "But let's not talk about her, tell me how you're doing?" she asked.

"Changing topics, eh?"

"Playing therapist again? Haha. O.K., so I want to avoid talking about her. Isn't that all right sometimes?" she asked playfully.

"We could drop the topic, but I do care about you. I'd like to know what happened."

"You are really too much, you know? I'm smiling right now, just so you know!" After a short pause she added, "I guess I can't say no to you."

"Ooooooooo, it really sounds like I have you wrapped around my finger doesn't it," he teased.

"Hey, I'm not so easy, Mister," she kidded in return.

"So tell me what happened. Come on, I want to know."

"O.K. O.K. This is not something I've told you much about," she began.

"Go on."

"My husband and my sister were very close."

"And?"

"And sometimes it bothered me. I mean, I don't think she would've ever done anything, but I always had these bothersome thoughts when we were all together. And there were times when I didn't know where he was, or rather, he was supposedly working late, and then I'd call my mother and find out my sister's kids were over because she'd gone out and my mother was babysitting. And so on. That kind of stuff."

"Wow," he replied and then paused.

"Wow? That's it?"

"That's some heavy stuff. I'm feeling bad for you."

Eileen hesitated. She was overwhelmed by her emotions and started to cry.

"Hello? You still there? Are you mad at me?" asked Sweetdude35, bewildered by her lack of responding.

Having wiped her eyes clear, Eileen noticed his typing and replied, "I'm not mad at you. This is just all sinking in right now. I just feel really bad, that's all. It's not you."

"Why don't we get together now? Why don't we have that cup of coffee we've talked about? Now is as good a time as any, don't you think?" he asked.

Eileen paused and rubbed her eyes again. At no point did she consider that this was *not* a good idea. She no longer thought of him as just a stranger out in cyberspace, or as untrustworthy. She liked him...liked him a lot. He knew a lot about her, and besides, what harm would come from meeting—in public, not alone. He wouldn't know where she lived. She wouldn't give out her phone number. She'd meet him somewhere away from here. It seemed exciting to her. He wasn't judgmental or critical or intrusive or opinionated... and he seemed to *really care*. The wine helped a bit, too.

After some time, she asked, "Where could we meet?"

"I thought I'd lost you for a second there. Well, you never told me where in New Jersey you're from? Do you want to work this out over the phone?"

"No. I don't want to give out my number."

"You feel comfortable enough to meet me in person but not comfortable enough to talk on the phone?" he asked, puzzled.

"It's different. I know it might seem arbitrary, but if we meet somewhere neutral I just feel it helps keep our privacy. And besides, what if I don't like you? Then I wouldn't want you harassing me on the phone, hahaha" she wrote, adding 'hahaha' to insure he understood it was meant tongue-in-cheek.

She had no fear at all that he would stalk her, or that he was some nut like the ones you read about in the papers. Still, she remained a tad unsure that this was the right thing to do. She was, however, feeling rather desperate and alone.

"Whatever you like. It doesn't make sense to me, but that's fine."

"How long would it take you to get to South Ridge Mall?" she asked.

"South Ridge? Are you serious?" he asked incredulously, a huge smile spanning his face.

"Why, is that too far?" asked Eileen.

"Too far? That's like twenty minutes from me. I can't fucking believe this."

"Hey, watch your mouth, you. I'm not interested in meeting with some garbage mouth (wink)."

"Oh, of course. I will treat you like a lady for sure," he replied. "Can you believe this?" he asked.

"Believe what?"

"We're chatting on the internet where you can meet anyone, anywhere, in any time zone and boom, by luck or destiny or whatever, two people from like no more than half an hour or an hour away from each other hook up like this. Don't you think it must mean something?"

"Well, I'm not into superstition or destiny or anything like that, if that's what you mean," she answered.

"Ah, well, it doesn't matter. Whatever the reason, this is incredible. It's so convenient. Haven't you read in the papers about people meeting online and then having to travel across the country to meet?"

"Yeah, those are the ones you read about because it's usually some maniac or sexual deviant," Eileen replied in jest, any hesitation or second thoughts having nearly vanished at this point. She felt comfortable with him and trusted her own instincts. But again, it was just words typed out, which failed to convey her lighthearted tone. Sweetdude35 misread her, and instead believed she was hedging.

"Oh come on, are you seriously worried about meeting me?" he asked.

"I'm joking. If I had any doubts about you I would have stopped chatting with you a long time ago. I think I am a pretty good judge of character. So when do you want to do this?"

"How's now?" he replied immediately.

"Now? The mall's not even open."

"Well we don't have to go into the mall. I thought we were just using that as a landmark. We can meet right in front of Macy's and then we'll find a diner or someplace where we can get coffee. Since the mall is closed we won't have any problem finding each other right in front."

"Hmmmmm...." Eileen typed, as she pondered this.

"Hmmmmm? Come on, no hmmmmm, let's just do it, otherwise we'll chicken out if we wait. Let's just go on our instincts," Sweetdude35 offered, trying his best to be persuasive.

Just as he finished typing there was a knock on his door. Without turning from the computer he called out, "Leave me the fuck alone! I'm busy."

His father replied, "I just need you for ten minutes. I need you to hold something up. I need your strength."

Sweetdude35 typed quickly, "Can you hold on one second. I'm being interrupted."

Then he got up from the computer, walked over to his door and without opening it, yelled to his father, "I said I'd fix the goddamned bookshelf myself. Can't ya leave it alone!"

"I'm not asking you to fix it. I'll do it. I'm going to take care of it. I just want you to hold up the side for two seconds and that's all I need. You won't have to work on it," replied his father through the door.

"Not right now. You'll have to wait like fifteen or twenty minutes, then I'll help ya, okay?"

"I wanted to go to bed, though. This will only take five minutes," his father pleaded, speaking as calmly as he could and trying to evoke some sympathy from his son. But his son ignored him and returned to the computer.

"Listen," he typed, "let's just do it. Let's meet now. I can be there in half an hour. How about you?"

A smile broke out on her face as she placed her fingers over the keyboard. She paused. She paused some more trying to think of just the right thing, and then simply decided on, "Let's go! I'll meet you right in front of Macy's in thirty minutes."

Overwhelmed with excitement, Sweetdude35 stood up and pumped a fist forward while letting out a slightly hushed "Yes!"

He sat back down and typed, "Let's do it. Thirty minutes to Macy's! Meet you then, Cheeryl."

And just as he finished typing, his father knocked again. Sweetdude35's excitement instantly transformed to rage, and he jumped from the computer and bounded to the door, unlocking and opening it to see his father still standing there.

"What the fuck is wrong with you?" he yelled. "I told ya I'd be ready in like fifteen minutes. Why the fuck are ya still standing here?"

"I wanted to go to bed. I just need you for like five minutes," offered his father, apologetically.

"Ya know what? Ya really fuckin' push me over the edge," Sweetdude35 raged. "You nag me, nag me, nag me. Ya act like you're giving me a break, 'Oh, just five minutes. I'm not asking much. I'm not asking you to do this,'" he said, mockingly. "But ya know, ya stand here pressuring me, pressuring me. Just forget about the fuckin' bookshelf, okay? Forget about it! Now I'm goin' out. Ya pissed me off, old man."

"Going out? Where? At this time?"

"What fuckin' difference does it make to you? Ya gonna ground me? I've got things to do. I'm goin' out." With that he barged passed his father and down the stairs, the door slamming behind him.

His father shook his head disgustedly as he stood for a moment at the threshold, listening to the car pulling away. His curiosity was piqued by what he saw in his son's bedroom. He entered the room like a visitor to a museum, looking up and around while stepping carefully and slowly. The bright computer screen attracted him most, as he stepped over clothes strewn on the floor and old bowls and plates with dried food scraps piled near the desk. He squinted as he leaned over to read, his lips silently mouthing the words:

Sweetdude35> How's now?

Cheeryl> Now? The mall's not even open.

Sweetdude35> Well we don't have to go into the mall. I thought we were just using that as a landmark. We can meet right in front of Macy's and then we'll find a diner or someplace to go get coffee. Since the mall is closed we won't have any problem finding each other right in front.

Cheeryl> Hmmmmm.....

Sweetdude35> Hmmmmm? Come on, no hmmmmm, let's just do it, otherwise we'll chicken out if we wait. Let's just go on our instincts.

His eyes moved down to the end where Cheeryl had ended the chat confirming to meet Sweetdude35 in thirty minutes, but wondering where his 'goodbye' was:

> *Cheeryl>* O.K. Half hour and I'll be there. See you then.
>
> *Cheeryl>* See ya.
>
> *Cheeryl>* You still there?
>
> *Cheeryl>* Hello??
>
> *Cheeryl>* O.K., I'll see you there. I hope you're not having second thoughts?
>
> *Cheeryl>* O.K. Bye.

As if by reflex, he reached down to the keyboard with one finger to press a few keys. He knew enough to understand that he was reading his son's online interactions with some stranger nicknamed "Cheeryl," and he wondered whether "Cheeryl" was still there and whether she'd react to his keystrokes. He was not bold enough to sit down and type away as if *he* were Sweetdude35, so he simply tapped out a few random keys:

Sweetdude35> wddffgfg

Immediately a message appeared, which assuaged a guilty feeling that had emerged over this mild transgression of his son's privacy:

Cheeryl is not logged on.

He decided not to snoop any further than he had—at least not right now—and he walked out of the room.

Chapter Eight

THE NIGHT WAS STILL AND MILD, BUT EILEEN WALKED TO HER CAR as though fighting gale force winds. She was battling herself: her heart said go, but her gut said no. She walked as if at any moment she might stop, turn around and run into the house, forgetting this whole stupid idea. She would just go back inside, go to bed and stay off the computer for the next month or so. He'd eventually leave her alone, she thought, if he didn't see her online for a long time. He'd give up on her. It doesn't matter what he'll think or how he'll feel four or five weeks from now. He didn't know her, or where she lived. And thank God she never gave him her phone number! It seemed capricious, earlier, when she explained why she would meet him in person but not give out her phone number. Meeting someplace in public away from home was safer, she believed. He can't harass her or stalk her, and if she decided now to turn around and go back inside, she would never have to face his disappointment, or his anger. That was the beauty of this online relationship, she thought. You can just leave it behind—shut it off—not face it. But she also knew he had given something to her life. He was there for her and listened to her in a way that no one else had. *He knows me. He knows the real me!*

There was no turning back.

Battling the excitement that propelled her to go on was a nagging inner voice telling her this was crazy and stupid and just plain *wrong*. For some reason she kept imagining what Michelle would say to her now. She pictured Michelle's face and its look of shock and incredulity. Michelle would *never* do anything like this. Maybe that's what made this so appealing. This was something that *Eileen* would never do either. This was *not* like Eileen. But Eileen didn't want to be Eileen anymore. She had spent her life pleasing others, and where had it gotten her? She wanted to please herself for once!

She pulled out of the driveway, her car moving with more speed and confidence than her walk. She just wanted to get there now; just get there and see what this guy looked like. The second-guessing was dimming now. She was excited about her little 'date.' *How was this any different than meeting someone from a personal ad? How was it different than any other blind date?* If a friend introduced you to a guy, and you arranged to go out for a drink or dinner, how safe would that be? Is that *really* any different from what she was doing, she thought.

She was lost in her thoughts as she drove down North Delano Turnpike toward South Ridge Mall. Her eyes fixed on the radio as *Endless Love* started playing. It was her and Ron's song. Maybe love was endless, she thought, just not with the same person. What a hypocrite that bastard was. It was *his* idea for the song, too. He wanted to have a family with her. He wanted to retire early so they could move to a warmer climate, maybe Georgia or South Carolina, but definitely not Florida. Oh yes, he was going to be the family man. Each year they would be the ones to host the holidays, he had said. Theirs would be the house where the others could gather. The families would come from all over to celebrate Thanksgiving and Christmas with Ron and Eileen, he'd planned. They would be the rock that others could turn to for support. It would always be that way, on and on and on, endlessly. What a happy loving couple growing old together, enjoying their golden years with their children and grandchildren. Endless love.

That's the way it was going to be; but that never happened. He was too selfish or ambitious or self-centered, and these plans were derailed long before they ever got started. He didn't want children, and the bastard convinced her that she didn't want them either. Moreover, the way things were going, she could have ended up in a marriage just like her mother's—battered, abused, put down, and alone. She changed the station before the song could further enrage her, searching the dial before finally shutting the radio off.

She pulled off Delano Turnpike and onto Commons way, the entrance road that heads directly to Macy's on the west side of the Mall. The stores had closed, and the parking lot was empty except for several cars scattered around. The silence in her car seemed loud with the radio off and her heart thumping loudly. She shivered, not from a chill but from nervousness, or maybe it was from excitement, or most likely from both. She felt as though she had to use the bathroom.

What would he look like? Would he be tall? Maybe he's just some fat, bald guy, she thought. *What good looking guy spends his time the way he did on the computer?*

There he is! She thought she spotted him, but no, her eyes or more probably her excitement was playing tricks on her. She pulled into a parking space and noticed someone walking through the lot right in front of Macy's, but it was just a young couple. She glanced toward the other side—her neck straining and her eyes squinting. *Could that be him against the wall?* She couldn't see well enough. *Maybe that was him! Oh God, how embarrassing it would be to ask some stranger if his name was Sweetdude!* In their haste to make this plan and in all their previous chatting, exchanging their real names never came up. He said she'd know it was him because no one else would be hanging outside the mall at this time. Well he was wrong, if you count the one couple that just walked by, she thought, the corners of her mouth pulling up slightly, betraying a smile. Maybe teasing him about that would be a good ice breaker, she thought, as she turned off her engine. She was sure that had to be him against the wall. There was no one else around. She got out of her car, shut the door and reflexively put the key in to lock it, as if she were now about to shop on a Saturday afternoon.

The silence of the parking lot was interrupted only by the clicking of her heels and the occasional whoosh of a car on Delano. Her heart raced. What would she say? She could see he wasn't fat, though she couldn't quite make out his facial features. He actually looked rather thin. Before she could see him clearly in the light he called out, "Cheeryl?" in what seemed like a familiar voice.

Thank God *he* took the risk of calling out the silly nickname, she thought. She was about ten yards from him when he moved forward and under one of the parking lot lights. She managed to reply "Sweetdude35," but swallowed "is that you?" in a gasp as she stood horrified and paralyzed, her entire body feeling as if it had just been dunked into ice water. She wasn't breathing. There was silence as they stared at each other. She felt weak, almost faint, shuddering at who she saw standing before her.

"Eileen *Duet?*" Brock Pagnotti finally said. But Eileen was frozen, her thoughts racing as panic ignited within her.

"Holy shit! Eileen Duet!" he said again.

"What are you *doing* here?!" she finally cried out. "What are you doing here? No! No! No! No! Oh God, no!" she shrieked, and immediately turned and began trotting quickly away from him and toward her car, as if she could now just run away from it. She was going to make it go away, but it was too late. She couldn't just shut the computer off now. She couldn't ignore it...but she ran, nonetheless.

"ME??? What the hell are you doin' here, Eileen Duet? *Cheeryl!*" he called out while jogging after her to the car. He emphasized 'Eileen Duet' and 'Cheeryl' as if ceremoniously unveiling her identity, and underscoring what this all meant.

"Get the hell away from me! Get away!" she screamed, and then she stopped momentarily to face him. "I'm going to call the police if you don't leave me alone. Do you hear me? I'll call the police!" she hollered.

Her face was soaked with tears, and mascara streaked down her pale cheeks. She turned around and began running toward her car. He continued after her.

"Call the police? Are you fuckin' crazy? You agreed to meet me here. Who the hell do ya think you are? You can't just blow me off like this."

"That wasn't you! Oh Gah-ah-ahd that wasn't you!" she stammered through her sobbing as she fumbled for her keys to unlock the car door. "This can't be happening. Please get away from me! Get away from me!" she screamed at him again and again.

Despite her protestations, she knew very well what she had done—that Sweetdude35 was Brock Pagnotti, and although this was a mistake, she had stupidly agreed to meet him and could not undo this tragic mistake.

"Don't you dare fuckin' blow me off like this. That was me," Brock persisted as he slid closer to her while holding her door shut with his hip. "You know it was me. Who the hell were ya meeting here, Eileen? Who? I'm Sweetdude, Eileen. Half an hour ago we agreed to meet, didn't we, *Cheeryl*? Where are ya running off to now? *I'm* that sweet guy you were talking to, Eileen. Ya can't pretend we didn't click, can ya? We had something together," he insisted.

She looked with horror at Pagnotti, her eyes widening as he spoke, and her stomach dropping when he said they had 'clicked'. She felt violated and sickened by his perception of this. She was afraid she would vomit right there. She wanted to die, to disappear; this couldn't possibly be happening! Their roles as therapist and patient were dissolved—the boundaries gone. The panic now worsening as little by little she realized the gravity of what had happened and the mistake she'd made. This was unreal. She could no longer hear him as her ears rang with the pounding of the pulse inside her head.

Every time she'd seen Pagnotti in therapy it was confined to the clinic. She walked him from the waiting area to her office, and that was it. She'd always kept her boundaries and her composure during sessions, no matter how his twisted and disturbed mind led him to ask all kinds of inappropriate questions about her personal life. And now here they stood together in a deserted parking lot having arranged to meet. *Oh what a terrible mistake!* Oh the things she had told him and confided in him! This was her *patient!* She stood there, her emotions reeling, having run from him, screaming, trying to make this all go away. And what was he thinking? that they *'clicked'*? Did he think that they would just work this out? She was appalled.

She pulled hard on the car door, lifting Pagnotti off and causing him to stumble back one step. "You're sick! SICK!" she screamed as she got into her car and slammed the door shut.

"Is that any way to talk to your patient?" Pagnotti replied sarcastically, though she most likely didn't hear him.

He turned and ran to his car as she drove off. He started it quickly and screeched out of his spot after her. He caught her at the first light as she turned onto North Delano Turnpike. There was one car between his and hers, but Eileen didn't notice him. She was focused on driving directly home as fast as she could. Her body was shivering, her teeth chattering as if she'd just stepped out of a shower. Thoughts streamed through her mind as she replayed—or rather, couldn't stop replaying—all of the confessions and private feelings and personal details she'd shared with him. She hadn't yet begun to think of the implications this would have for her at work. Pagnotti was a patient of hers, and he very likely had a scheduled appointment for some time this week. He was almost *always* seen weekly. But these implications hadn't surfaced just yet. Instead, she was suffocating under the overwhelming humiliation of what she did tonight and what she had done over the past several months.

She arrived at her street, Birchwood Lane, which had large homes scattered here and there separated by rather large property. She slowed as she approached her driveway and only then noticed the headlights behind her. She thought momentarily that it was peculiar to see another car this close to her on Birchwood. There wasn't another driveway for at least forty or so yards. *This is odd.* She got out of her car and nearly collapsed when she realized the headlights belonged to Brock Pagnotti's car. He had followed her home! Oh my God! she thought, but she was frozen. Her legs shook. She was shaking so severely, her upper body was vibrating.

"D-d-don't you d-d-dare c-c-come any closer! You...you're stalk... this is harassment, Brock—"

"Harassment to follow my *date* home, when she agreed to meet me? My *therapist* date, that is? Will ya be telling the police that I'm your patient and you agreed to—"

"STOP IT! STOP IT! I don't want to hear that," she yelled as she moved cautiously backwards toward her front door. She stepped gingerly and slowly as if any sudden movement would startle or provoke him.

He seemed much calmer than he normally was in sessions, but there was an unusual eeriness to his demeanor. He smirked slightly, but his eyes seemed disconnected from emotion as he seemed to stare through her. It was a look she had never before seen in him. He moved forward, one step at a time and then pausing in between while she backed up continuously, creeping ever so slightly back toward her house.

"I'm not going to hurt ya, Eileen. I'm not like your husband," he said, a sinister smile breaking out across his face.

"Brock, please, STOP! Just stop right there and we'll talk. Please don't come any closer," she pleaded.

"We have something very special, Eileen. You were able to get to know the real me like no one ever got to know me. We didn't know what the other one looked like. We didn't have any preconceived ideas about one another. We connected, babe; you can be sure of that. You told me how sweet I was, didn't ya?"

"Brock, that was fantasy. I didn't know who I was talking to, don't you see? You can be anyone you want to be online. People make things up. It's not real. They create an image," she argued.

"Well *I* wasn't making anything up. That was the real me, Eileen. And if ya didn't like who ya were chatting with, or if ya thought I was some kind of phoney or nut job, then why the *hell* would you agree to meet me in person? Huh? Why? Explain that one to me." And as he finished he took several more steps toward her. Eileen turned and ran up the walkway. She ran as if being chased, though Brock had stopped and was simply enjoying the sense of control he had and the fear he could now inflict on her.

Just as she got into the house, she looked back and paused, realizing the safe distance between them as he remained standing in the driveway. "Go away, now, Brock. I'm calling the police. You better go," she cried out, and then she shut the door.

She stood momentarily leaning against the front door, feeling somewhat safer inside now. The house was quiet. After a few seconds she spun around and peaked out the narrow windows that framed the front door, wanting to insure that he was leaving, although she had no intention of calling the police. Brock was just climbing back into his car. His headlights came on and the engine turned over. He was driving away. Relief. Her heart was still pounding, her breathing shallow and rapid. She was feeling sick. The feeling came quite suddenly. Nausea. She dropped her keys on the floor and stepped quickly into the bathroom to vomit.

Chapter Nine

FUELED BY ADRENALINE, PAGNOTTI PRESSED THE GAS PEDAL TO THE floor as he headed home, toying now and then with the idea of turning around and reappearing at her doorstep. That would freak her out, he thought, and he cackled aloud to himself, which caused his car to nearly serve off the road. This had been an incredible evening. He decided to continue home without turning around and going back, but not because he thought she'd call the police. There was no way she'd call the police. How could she? She was his therapist and *she* agreed to meet him there. She'd be the one who would have a lot of explaining to do. He didn't force her or coerce her or threaten her in any way. And he had *all* their chat sessions saved on his computer! If anyone needed proof of his relationship with her, he had all the evidence he needed. "Whooo-hoooo!" he crowed, and he slapped his steering wheel as if giving it a high five.

His thoughts swirled as he reminisced about a mix of this evening's events together with bits and pieces of their previous chat sessions: *How sweet you are! Why are you so good to me? If you were my therapist, I'd owe you so much money.* If I were her therapist, he thought. *If I were her fuckin' therapist!!* he mumbled aloud in disbelief. *Holy shit! Un-fucking-believable!*

Lost in his thoughts, he sat at an intersection for half a minute after the light changed to green. A car behind him began honking repeatedly. Startled out of his musing, Pagnotti glanced at his rear view mirror, then at the green traffic light before pounding the accelerator and screeching away.

Cruising along at about fifty miles per hour in a thirty-five mile per hour zone, he was back to his thoughts. He couldn't believe the personal details he'd learned about her. He couldn't believe the person he'd been chatting with (*counseling!*) was his therapist. By day she was counseling him, and by night he was counseling *her!* How ironic! *How fuckin' ironic is that?* She had confided in him about her failing marriage, and about her abusive husband; but more importantly, he thought, she *craved* his support. (*She told me how sweet I am!*) And *that* was the *real* him. The real 'him' was not the person she knew in therapy, he believed. The person he was online was caring and supportive—*a good listener!* She told him so. Yes, this would work out in the long run, he was sure. She just needed some time.

When he pulled into his driveway and turned the car off, he thought it strange that the light in the family room was still on because his father usually went to bed before ten. *God, was he still up working on the damn bookshelf?* He entered the house and found his father, still awake, lying on the couch in front of the TV.

"Hey, you're back," said his father, grunting as he slowly lifted his tired body to a sitting position. "I finished the bookshelf. Would ya like—"

"I told ya before I don't give a fuck about the bookshelf," Brock interrupted. Then he flung his keys on the coffee table and stormed into the kitchen, his father following in silence a safe distance behind.

"Did you have a good time tonight?" his father asked cautiously.

"What is that supposed to mean?" asked Brock brusquely, now glaring at his father.

"Well, I...uh...it basically means...well, just what I said. You know...whatever you did when you left tonight...did you enjoy yourself," replied Mr. Pagnotti, stammering as he did his best not to rile his son's anger.

"*Why* are you askin' that? I'm not askin' ya to restate your question. I know *what* ya said. I'm not deaf. What I'm askin' is *why* you're asking me that? I go out many nights. Why is this different? What is it ya think I was doin' that ya need to know if I had a good time?"

Like a bloodhound, Brock's suspicious mind had caught a whiff of something in the way his father was talking to him. He sauntered menacingly toward his father until he was hovering over him, his scowling face jutted forward. His father retreated back several steps.

"Awww, come on now, Brock, you're always so damned paranoid," he began, trying to lighten the moment. He shrugged his shoulders and threw his hand forward in a dismissive gesture as he continued, "You're making too much of this. Come on, it's late. Why don't we both call it a night." And he turned and began to walk away.

But Brock grabbed him by the shoulder and spun him around. "Listen, ya little shit! I don't know what kind of mind games you're up to now, or why you're trying to fuck with me, but let's just cut the shit, okay? Do ya understand?" he bellowed.

"Brock, I understand. I understand. I'm not playing any games. I promise you. Forget what I said, please. It's not a big deal. Let's go to bed, please?" his father pleaded meekly.

Brock, still sneering, dropped his hand from his father's shoulder. Without another word from either of them, Mr. Pagnotti slipped away and up the stairs breathing a great sigh of relief. At least he hadn't hit him or pushed him, he thought. It was clear that he was sensitive about this new person in his life, the one he was chatting with online; that was obvious by the way he jumped all over his question. Maybe this relationship (*or friend or whoever she was*) would be a good thing for him. Maybe she would soften him up a bit, he thought. *Ahhh, who could ever soften up that bastard with his sick and twisted mind?* As soon as she gets to know him or sees a hint of that temper of his, she'd be out of his life, he thought. And with those final considerations, Mr. Pagnotti climbed into bed and was quickly asleep.

Eileen awoke the next morning with her head throbbing. She sat up, leaning on her elbows, and looked out the window. It was raining hard and the wind whipped through the few remaining leaves on the trees. The windows shook. Nothing but the pain in her head was on her mind until she noticed the clock radio and, realizing it was time to get up for work, her stomach knotted up. A wave of panic passed through her, stopping in the pit of her gut.

She had slept well, but now the images of last night flooded her mind. How could she be so stupid? She felt trapped. Her heart pounded. Would he tell somebody? Or would he just harass her now? How could she continue to see him in therapy? Could she simply confess this mistake to her supervisor? Was her license in jeopardy? How could she possibly explain her bad judgment? *I was under a lot of stress,* she reasoned, and that's why she did it. *My husband had been killed in an accident, and who knows what my sister was up to with him. My mother was of no help, and in fact made things worse. I had no one to turn to. They're all mental health professionals; they'd understand, wouldn't they?*

I had no one! No one! she thought as she collapsed back down into the bed covering her face with her hands as she cried in despair. After several minutes, she looked again at the clock. There was no way she could call in sick after all the time she'd already taken.

She eventually made her way out of bed and into the shower. The nervousness in her stomach never left; it was constant now and had obliterated her appetite. She finished showering, dressed and walked downstairs. She pulled her umbrella out of the closet and stepped outside into the blustery October morning. In the car, she played the radio loud to drown out her thoughts, but it failed to help. Nothing helped. She was so nervous she felt nauseous again, but it subsided as she pulled into the clinic parking lot. She took a few slow, deep breaths, steadied herself and got out of her car.

As soon as she arrived in her office and closed the door, there was a knock. Michelle opened the door and stuck her head in without waiting for an invitation.

"Hey, how ya feeling?"

"No, I'm fine. Really, everything's okay."

"Well, Eileen," Michelle continued, closing the door behind her, "you're looking a little...under the weather. Is that the right expression? God, I know that sounds so corny coming out of my mouth. I don't think I've ever used that expression 'under the weather' before. But—"

"Michelle, I'm fine, okay?" Eileen replied curtly, her eyes noticeably averting Michelle's face. There was silence for a moment, as Eileen made it clear she was uninterested in talking. Persistent as always, and oblivious to Eileen's body language, Michelle sat down and pulled her chair closer to Eileen, whose eyes remained on the floor.

"Eileen, I'm here for you."

"I don't *need* anyone to be here for me. I'm perfectly capable of taking care of myself, Michelle."

"Eileen, you lost your husband. You're entitled to have these feelings—"

"Michelle, I didn't ask for you to counsel me. Please! Just stop!" Eileen demanded with an uncharacteristically loud voice. Again there was silence. Michelle stared at Eileen, whose head remained partially turned toward her bookcase.

After another minute, Eileen stood up, walked to the window, and again raised her voice at Michelle, "You all think this is so easy, don't you. Everyone's got an answer."

"Who 'all', Eileen?"

"People make mistakes, Michelle, you know? Maybe you can't understand this. Maybe life is just too damn easy for you."

"Eileen?"

"Yeah, when things are nice and easy and going smoothly, it's very easy just to take a deep breath or 'get a different perspective.'" Then turning and facing Michelle, whose stunned eyes were as wide as her mouth, she shouted, "I'm NOT perfect, Michelle. I'm sorry, okay?"

"You have nothing to be sorry about, Eileen," she said softly, but Eileen ignored her. A tense, awkward silence followed. Michelle bowed her head contritely as Eileen sat back down.

Michelle finally stood up and walked to the door. "Eileen, I'm sorry if whatever I've said or done has caused you to feel...to feel some...some pressure or whatever. That's not what I intended. I'm not sure I'm following everything you're talking about. I just want you to know I care, okay?"

Without waiting for a reply, she walked out the door.

Eileen sat back down at her desk, the heavy rain outside pelting the window. Her stomach was tight, her breathing shallow, and her knees shaking. She reached for a pen with a shaky hand but the phone rang.

"Hello?"

"Eileen?

"Yes?

"Pagnotti's calling. He has an appointment for next Monday that he wants to move up to this week. I was going to—"

"Pagnotti's on the phone now?" Eileen interrupted.

"Yes, I have him on hold," replied Mary. "I was going to put him in your Friday slot at eleven because your supervision was canceled."

"Mary?"

"Yes?"

"Pagnotti's on the phone *now*?"

"Yes. You just asked me that," replied Mary, rather puzzled.

"What did he say?"

"I told you, he's just calling to...Are you okay, Eileen?"

"Yes...I'm okay."

"He's not doing so well. He just wanted to move up his appointment, so I'm putting him in for Friday. Is that all right?"

"That's all he wants, Mary?" asked Eileen, her stomach and shoulders so tight they felt as if they were on fire.

"Eileen, he's just calling to move his appointment up. I know he's a pain in the ass, but you're sounding way too stressed out over this," Mary responded with an uneasy laugh.

"That's fine. That's fine, Mary. Go ahead and schedule it. I'm sorry. I'm just not...it's okay. Whatever's available; go ahead and set it up."

Eileen hung up, her breathing so rapid and shallow she was beginning to hyperventilate. How could she see him now? How? How could she face him? What was she going to do? Could she just go ahead and see him and tell him to forget about what happened? What was he going to say? Would he blackmail her? Would he try to force her to do something with the threat of revealing what happened? Couldn't she just say it was a mistake? It was stupid, but it was just a mistake. She didn't know it was him, and besides, nothing happened after they met. She left him immediately when she realized who it was. Nothing happened! She should tell Dr. Thomas, she thought; that would be the right thing to do. No, she couldn't. This would be way too embarrassing. Oh God! she thought. *I want to die. I want to just die. I can't stand how this feels.*

Over the next several days, Eileen walked through the motions of seeing her patients, though she continued to fall far behind in her paperwork, something that was uncharacteristic of her. She called several patients by the wrong name, and on one occasion she began asking a question that had to do with a case she was thinking about, but had no relevance to the patient sitting in front of her. She apologized, simply stating to the rather befuddled patient that the "the story was confusing."

Eileen's mother called several times expressing concern that she was isolating from her and from her sister. "Your family is all you have in life, Eileen," she told her. But Eileen remained mostly silent. She had lost ten pounds on her already thin frame and on at least two occasions had skipped taking a shower for as long as two days, something she'd never done before. By Friday her body felt beaten up—she was weak, shaky, and so anxious that she felt disconnected from her body and her surroundings. She thought about cutting herself with a razor or a kitchen knife just so she could feel something—anything—other than this anxiety.

There was no way to avoid the inevitable: she would have to see Pagnotti at some time, whether now or a week from now or ten days from now. There was no reasonable way—short of confessing this self-created mess to her supervisor—to keep this from unfolding. Maybe—just maybe—she thought she could still keep the situation from unraveling. She didn't want to lose her job, or worse, her license. She didn't want anyone to find out about this, or for this *scandal* to make the local papers. Oh God! This *is* a scandal, she thought. This was horrible, just horrible. She imagined how the newspapers would exploit the story: *Therapist has Internet Liaison with Patient! Therapist Resigns after Online and Offline Hookup with Her Patient,* and *Therapist Stripped of License after Cyberspace Dalliance with Patient* were just a few of the imagined headlines that flooded her mind as she ruminated. Her face was sunken around the mouth, her dark eyes swelled from crying, and her skin had a blotchy red rash just below her jaw and down the left side of her neck.

Any number of things *could* happen, but it was also possible that Pagnotti himself was embarrassed or feeling uneasy about this unfortunate and freak set of circumstances. After all, Pagnotti had hundreds of other issues and problems that could preoccupy him, she figured. But the fact that he moved his appointment up was a bad sign.

Eleven o'clock arrived and as expected Pagnotti arrived almost exactly on the hour. Eileen had remained in her office for the entire first two hours of the morning, avoiding everyone, and ignoring her backlog of unfinished paperwork. She sat staring out the window, at her bookshelf, and at her desk. Occasionally she stood and paced the floor. She felt sick.

The phone rang.

"Eileen, your eleven o'clock is here," announced Mary in a matter-of-fact tone.

"Mary, that's Pagnotti, right?"

"Yep."

A few seconds passed without a reply. Then Mary spoke up, "Eileen?"

"Yes. Yes. I'm here, Mary."

"Mr. Pagnotti is here."

"Okay, I'll be right out."

She walked on her unsteady legs out of the office and down the hallway to the waiting area where Pagnotti was standing—as usual. He never sat in the waiting area with the other patients. It was as if he wanted to insure that anyone seeing him there wouldn't consider him one of *them*—one of the *mental* patients, which is another reason he always wore suits to his sessions. He frequently referred to the patients in the waiting area as 'sickos' or 'wackos' or 'crazies'; he saw himself as different from them.

His grandiosity left little room for tolerating other people's quirks or differences, and he would often resort to name-calling and other forms of verbal abuse when others didn't behave according to his rules. She thought of this now, as she approached him in the waiting room, because she was experiencing an anxiety-provoking recollection—much like a flashback—of one of their recent online chats. When she thought her anonymous online partner was just a sympathetic listener, he had told her that her husband needed to develop more flexible 'rules' about other people's conduct so that he wasn't always "flying off the handle when others didn't meet his rigid expectations." She was struck by his insight then. Some insight, she thought now. Here she was spilling her guts to him about intimate details regarding her marital problems, and he was 'counseling' her with recycled phrases *she* had used with him regarding *his own* anger problems. *How humiliating it was!* How weak and vulnerable and embarrassed she felt standing before him.

"Mr. Pagnotti?" she offered, barely audibly.

"Ah, it's good to see you," he replied as he spun around to greet her with an unusually cheerful smile.

Eileen led him to her office, closed the door behind them and sat down stiffly at her desk. Pagnotti broke the silence immediately, which was a good thing because Eileen's perplexed and dazed mind was a complete blank.

"Ya haven't been online at all since our meeting. I was hopin' that maybe that was a way we could talk about this, since that's where we really connected, ya know?"

"Brock, I don't want to talk about this again beyond what we say here and now," she began, her voice quivering noticeably. "I did something very stupid...exceptionally stupid. Even therapists can use bad judgment. But we have to learn from—"

"Wait, wait, wait. I'm not exactly likin' what I'm hearin' here," said Pagnotti, shifting and twitching with annoyance in his seat. "Are ya gonna sit here and tell me to my face that ya didn't have feelin's for the guy ya *thought* ya were chatting with? Cuz ya know that's a lie, Eileen."

"Brock, listen. I *enjoyed* the conversations, but it's not about what 'feelings' you or I had. It was about conversations—chatting. We were two people chatting to someone we thought was just another stranger out there. It was fantasy—"

"THAT'S SHIT, AND YOU KNOW IT! This is bullshit, Eileen. You confided in me! You agreed to meet with me! The fantasy is over when you decide to meet. That's not fantasy, Eileen, that's reality."

Eileen shuddered at his words, as it became clear that no matter how she attempted to downplay or dismiss what happened, he was clearly stuck, seeing this in much more significant and dramatic terms. He tried to convince her that rather than dismiss what happened, they instead should pursue it and develop it. This argument sickened her; even worse, it terrified her. What would he do if he felt rejected? How far was he willing to push this?

Eileen was hyperventilating, and she was shivering as if the room was freezing. Pagnotti stood up and approached her.

"I want to help ya get through this difficult time, Eileen. I want to have that cup of coffee ya promised me."

He reached out with the index finger of his left hand attempting to lift her chin upward, as one might do to a child who was sulking. Her head jerked toward her left shoulder.

"Brock, please...sit...please sit down...sit back down," she requested, her heart pounding so hard it seemed to shake her vocal chords as she spoke. He smiled, as his anger seemed to melt into the pleasure he took in terrorizing her.

"Ya know what I'm wonderin' about, Eileen?" he said, pulling his hand away and turning his back as if he were now going to enjoy a stroll through what little office space she had. "I'm wonderin' what other people might think about your sudden—"

"Other people? What other people, Brock? What do you mean?" Eileen pressed him desperately.

"I mean..." He looked at her and then paused, the eerie serenity of his earlier demeanor quickly giving way to his typical hostility. "I mean, who the hell are you to play games with my feelings, huh?? You're always so goddamned self-righteous, aren't ya? Oh yeah, I'm the one makin' somethin' out of this, right? I'm the dope who didn't realize this was just a 'fantasy,' or that we were just chatting, right? Well FUCK YOU!" he boomed, and then again, "FUCK YOU! I'd really like to know what other people will think if they read our little chats. I wonder if they'd come to the same conclusion that I came to. Or if they'd somehow conclude that this was just fun and games."

Prior thoughts that he *may have* saved the text of just *some* of their chats did not nearly concern her as much as the dread that now filled her as she immediately realized he very likely saved the text of *all* of their chats. That would be just like him, she thought. *He probably even has some of our dialogue memorized! Oh God, this is awful!*

"Brock, why do you need to save that stuff? It's just going to upset you m—"

"SHUT UP! SHUT YOUR MOUTH!" he commanded, and he grabbed her chin between his forefinger and thumb, aggressively jerking her head up and into his eyes as stared down at her. "I am that sweet guy, ya got to know online. This therapy isn't goin' anywhere without us talking about this, *Cheeryl*. You're not just blowin' me off, babe, because I haven't felt like this in a long time...a long time! And I'm likin' our little online romance very much. And now that we've taken it to the next level, I'm not lettin' ya just blow me off. Do ya hear me? I'm not gonna fuckin' let you just blow me off like I'm a nobody!"

Eileen was immobile. Her eyes widened, frozen on her tormentor as he clutched her jaw more tightly in his hand. Then he let go of her chin, and just as quickly as his temper had flared, he now tenderly brushed her hair from her forehead, leaned down and pressed his lips on her head.

He walked away, opened the door and stopped. He turned around and before walking out said to her, "Check your email, hon. Let's keep in touch, okay?"

Eileen's face was pale. She sat motionless for several minutes, traumatized. She couldn't cry. She couldn't breathe. Again she was hyperventilating, gasping for air, her fingers clutching the ends of the chair arms; her mouth and throat were parched, her head throbbing and her surroundings seeming to swirl around her. She felt a tingling sensation down the side of her face and in her fingertips. Her skin seemed to alternate between ice and fire. She feared she was going to pass out. Finally, she fell forward onto the floor.

Chapter Ten

WHEN JEREMY, THE PSYCHOLOGY INTERN WHO OCCUPIED THE office adjacent to Eileen's, heard her patient slam the door shut and leave, his curiosity (or maybe just plain nosiness) got the better of him. He held his ear against her door as he knocked, his eyes darting wildly around him.

"Eileen? Eileen? Eileen, are you okay?" he called through the door with a loud, throaty whisper, trying his best to be inconspicuous and wondering if he were overreacting to the loud voices and shouting he thought he heard coming from her office. Unable to contain his curiosity, he turned the doorknob and pushed the door open just enough to allow himself to wrap his long neck around to poke his head in.

"Eileen! Eileen, what's the matter? Are you okay?" he cried as he dashed to her on the floor where, on hands and knees, she appeared to be either searching for a contact lens or trying to stand. He supported her right arm and held her hand as he lifted and guided her back onto her chair.

"Eileen, what happened? Are you feeling okay?"

"Jeremy, I'm fine; I'm fine," Eileen whispered, shaking her head gently as if to put her jumbled thoughts back in order. "Nothing happened.... Everything's O.K.... I was just feeling a little lightheaded, that's all. I think maybe I need something to eat."

Jeremy picked up the phone and began to dial.

"What are you doing? Who are you calling?" exclaimed Eileen. "Put the phone down, please," she demanded, knocking over a cup of pencils as she reached over to grab the phone away.

"You should really get checked out, Eileen," Jeremy insisted. "You don't just faint from being hungry...." He paused and then asked with suspicious, squinting eyes, "Did he hurt you, Eileen?"

"'He'? He who, Jeremy?"

"Pagnotti. You just had a session with him and I heard him shouting. Did he—"

"Jeremy, you heard us through the walls?" Eileen blurted out as the color drained from her face.

"I wasn't listening in; you guys were loud," he answered defensively.

"What did you hear, Jeremy. Tell me what you heard!" she begged.

"Take it easy, Eileen. Are you okay?"

"Jeremy, I'm fine, but I don't want you mentioning this to anyone, okay?" she pleaded. "I'm just...I-I'm...well you know with what's happened recently with my husband's accident and all. Well, I don't know, you know—I just haven't been taking good care of myself; I haven't been eating. So I was...I was just a little woozy this morning, that's all. That's all it is, Jer. This is embarrassing, you know, so please don't mention this to anyone, Jeremy. Can you please?"

But Jeremy stood expressionless and showed no sign of agreement as Eileen struggled to construct this flimsy explanation. She looked frail and petrified, her pupils receding into the whites of her widening eyes. Something was wrong, he was sure, but he couldn't understand why she'd lie to him or wouldn't want help. He was suspecting that Pagnotti had hurt her, but how, he wondered. And why wouldn't she want anyone to know? What were they arguing about, and why in the world would she be on the floor? Had Pagnotti been on the floor with her, he wondered. Ah, that's ridiculous, he thought, and he dismissed these speculations immediately.

He respected Eileen's seniority and experience, and if she didn't want him talking about this, she must have a good reason. An intern couldn't press the issue any further, he figured. Still, he thought, how odd it was for her to be on the floor, and even stranger yet how she vehemently insisted he keep quiet. He looked at her, bit his lip and very deliberately shook his head.

"Jeremy, can you just tell me what you heard? What did you hear Pagnotti say?" she implored him, which only served to raise his suspicions.

"Eileen, that guy is whacked. We all know that. Did he—"

"Forget about what we know, Jeremy. I know he's *whacked*. I'm just asking what you heard," she screeched as she grabbed his wrists with both hands.

Jeremy's eyes widened and his head shot back as he pulled his hands away. "Relax! It was nothing, Eileen. I just heard loud voices and I got concerned. You can't hear through the walls, but when someone is loud like that, well...you can hear it. You hear the loud voices, but I didn't hear what was being said. Jeez, Eileen, I was worried about you. I'm sorry; I apologize for rushing in here like that."

"No, no, no, no, Jeremy. You don't have to apologize. I should apologize. You did the right thing. Hell, for all you knew I could have been having a heart attack," she said, pushing her hair behind her ears and then rubbing her mouth with the back of her hand.

She took a deep breath and strained to produce a smile. "No, I'm glad you came in—I'm just embarrassed, that's all. So I'd really wish you'd just keep this to yourself, okay?" she asked, but her wrinkled forehead and quivering chin belied her reassurances and left Jeremy unconvinced.

"Whatever, Eileen, that's fine. No problem...I guess...I guess I'll see ya, then" he replied as he walked out.

Eileen sat staring at the ceiling for a moment, her thoughts piling one on top of the other—wondering whether Jeremy would tell Dr. Thomas and start gossiping about this to the staff? And what should she do with Pagnotti's therapy now? Should she spread out his sessions to see him less often? Would it be possible to finish treatment with him and close his case? Or maybe she could tell him she's going away for awhile and then close his case? No, that's just crazy, she thought.

But no matter how preposterous her ideas, she couldn't halt the desperate thoughts and images that deluged her. Her mind raced from one catastrophic thought to another. She felt guilty and embarrassed—her world was spinning out of control. But Eileen was masterful at ignoring problems that swirled about her, and she could press on as if all was okay. For this ability, she credited being raised by a violent drunken father; it prepared her well for a lifetime of denial and excuses.

Eileen functioned, but she wasn't eating or sleeping. She smiled when she had to, spoke when spoken to, feigned a wide range of emotions to get through the day; but underneath, her emotions roiled.

As the week wore on, she obsessed on what she thought others were saying or thinking about her. Did they consider her behavior strange? Was she unusually aloof today? Were they whispering to each other about her appearance, or about her lack of makeup? Or her hair being tied back again? She went out of her way to make small talk with support staff, to act as if everyday was just an average day at the office, but her efforts seemed forced and clumsy.

On the weekend, Eileen resumed sorting through her husband's belongings at home. She had left this task for a long while, but knew that nothing helped better to constrain her fears and block her crazy thoughts than keeping busy with thoughtless activity. To sit and watch TV or to read or even to get to bed early would only invite the torrent of ruminations that flooded her mind. She was falling to pieces ever so slowly, day by day. Busy work helped to slow it down by creating the illusion she was in control of something.

Most of the upstairs had been cleaned out by this time. She had given away his clothes and taken a number of boxes from home to his workplace. Tonight she went down the basement to sort through his work area. Ron was a klutz with his hands and usually hired others to fix things around the house. But never short on machismo, Ron had to have the biggest, best and most expensive tool kit, the latest mechanical innovations, all the gizmos and gadgets and devices and electronics—all to swell his ego and engender his buddies' envy.

The work area down the basement looked nearly undisturbed, as if he hadn't ever worked there, and she was tempted to leave it alone. After all, she thought, when she finally got around to selling the house this would certainly be one of the highlights. As she was walking around to decide where to start, her attention was drawn to the far edge of a low shelf near the corner of the basement. At the end of the shelf lay an envelope, two screws, a crumpled piece of paper, a neatly folded one, and a napkin, partially hidden underneath a large sheet of sandpaper. It caught her eye because it was the only area that was even slightly out of order. Eileen first intended to straighten the area and throw out the napkin and papers, but as she stooped over and reached to pick up the pile, the sandpaper and screws fell to the floor and she was left holding the napkin and the neatly folded paper. Noticing Ron's name penciled on the front of the paper, she unfolded it to see what it said.

Babe,

I'm sorry I put you through that. I promise it won't happen again. Let's just put this behind us and forget about it. Hey, if you're a 'good boy' I'll make it up to you on the weekend. (wink) Kisses.

Love,
Kelly

Stunned, Eileen read and re-read the message several times. Her breathing was fast, shallow and halting; her lips pressed tightly together; she felt her pulse throb in her forehead. After a long pause, she folded the paper and hurried up the stairs. She grabbed her coat and keys and rushed to see her sister, whom she hadn't seen or spoken to in weeks.

She pulled into Kelly's driveway and despite not seeing her car, charged up to the door and started knocking. Then she banged her fist against the door and yelled for her, but there was no answer. She had visions of choking her sister when she came to the door, or slapping or punching her, or simply throwing the note in her face and walking away; she was livid and wanted to hurt her. She didn't know what to do with these feelings because rage of this magnitude had never managed to surface in her—ever. Her knocking and banging on the door were futile; no one was home, so she walked back to her car and sat, nostrils flaring and eyebrows drawn tightly together.

After five minutes, she fumbled with trembling fingers for the note in her pocket. She read it once more, crumpled it in a clenched fist and pounded her thigh as she began to cry.

Fifteen minutes had passed when Kelly's Jeep, horn beeping twice to cheerfully announce her arrival, pulled into the driveway alongside Eileen's car. As each climbed out of her car to greet one another, Eileen's private rage and imagined bravado were thrust aside by her usual restraint, which was rooted in a deep-seated fear of conflict. She still trembled, but now felt weak, unsure, and overwhelmed by a desire to turn around, run and hide. Noticing Eileen's tears, Kelly asked, "Hey, what's the matter? What's going on?"

"We need to talk, Kel," Eileen muttered, her arms folded tightly across her chest and eyes riveted straight ahead as Kelly, glancing back every so often with a puzzled expression but saying nothing, led her sister into the house.

"Can I get you something to drink or eat? You look like you've lost weight, 'leenie. Is everything all right?"

"Kelly, we need to talk about Ron," Eileen burst out, choking on her words as she fought back tears. Kelly closed the cabinet where she had reached for a bag of Oreos and turned slowly to look at her sister.

"I just can't believe this," Kelly began in a measured tone. "I cannot believe he's gone. I know exactly what you're going through, hon, I know. It's going to get—"

"That's not why I'm here, Kelly. That's not why..." said Eileen, but she started to cry and was unable to finish speaking. "That's not why I'm here," she tried again, her head down and forehead pressed against the palms of her hands, her elbows tucked into her stomach as she curled over as though she were sick.

"Eileen! What's the matter, hon? It's okay. It's okay," Kelly reassured her as she sat down and leaned over just a bit to try to make eye contact. Eileen pulled away, reached into her pocket and shoved the note onto the table.

"What is—" Kelly began, but then caught her words in her throat as she saw her own handwriting. "Where did you get this, Eileen?"

Eileen, her face wrinkled with a mix of disbelief, bitterness and disgust, looked up at her sister's stunned, pale face and asked, "Where did I get this? That's what you want to know, Kelly? Where did I get this? Is that what matters to you?"

"Eileen, I...I don't know what to say. This isn't what you're...I hope you're not thinking...Eileen, listen to me. This was a joke. It was an inside jo—"

"Stop, Kelly. Just stop. You're embarrassing us both," Eileen shouted as she stood up and stormed out of the kitchen. Kelly chased after her to the front door.

"Eileen, can we just talk about this? For God sakes, you're a goddamned therapist, can we just talk about this so you can understand some things?"

"I can't look at you right now, Kelly. I CAN'T LOOK AT YOU, YOU SON OF A BITCH! I HATE YOU!" she screamed. "I lost my husband, and now I've lost my sister," she said as she continued out the door. Kelly kept pace behind, hurrying after her sister, who was climbing back into her car now.

"You can really be dramatic, Eileen. This is really dramatic," she called out. "Can we at least talk?" But Eileen had slammed the door shut and was pulling out of the driveway.

Eileen caught herself several times swerving into the opposite lane as she drove away, tears streaming down her face. She thought for awhile that she would be better off dead. She wished she could go to sleep and not wake up. It was becoming more and more difficult to face the world, and she felt she had no one left to turn to. She felt humiliated by what her sister and husband had done. What conversations had they had about her as they planned their furtive meetings; what had he confided in her; what personal matters had he shared? She felt betrayed, ashamed, laid bare, and angry.

She arrived home just as it was beginning to rain and the wind was picking up. She got out of her car and ran inside. The house was cold so she turned the heat up, before tossing her coat on the sofa and sliding her shoes off. It had been weeks since she had cleaned or straightened the house. It was October and with the wide swings in temperature over the past three weeks, she now had several different jackets and coats tossed haphazardly on the sofa. The house was a mess.

She went into the kitchen to pour a glass of wine and to get a cigarette lighter. Then she walked into the study where the computer remained untouched since her meeting with Pagnotti in the parking lot outside Macy's. She felt a momentary urge to smash it, as if the computer was the cause of the crisis she now faced. She gulped the wine until it was finished, then poured another glass, stopping only to light a cigarette in between.

It wasn't long ago that the computer served as a respite for her, an excursion into a world that allowed her easy contact with others and a break from the miserable relationship she had to endure. Up until now she had successfully avoided the computer, but with a little wine and the lighting of her cigarette, the old feelings began to crystallize, and she felt it's temptation heighten.

Her curiosity was too much to resist. She sat down and turned it on hurriedly, as if she needed to take advantage of this sudden urge before it passed. She wasn't sure what she needed to do or why she was doing it now, but she felt compelled. She planned only to check her email and log off. There would be no chatting tonight; there would never be any chatting again, she swore to herself.

The computer completed its beeps and chimes and hissing sounds and then fell silent. Her eyes remained glued to the screen while she took a final drag on her cigarette. She paused for a moment, then determinedly began pointing and clicking to log on and retrieve her email.

A chill ran from the base of her neck all the way down her back as the computer completed downloading the email: Thirty-six of the thirty-eight messages were from Sweetdude35! He was harassing her, stalking her! she thought. She wanted to delete them without reading, but this proved impossible. She needed to know what state of mind he was in. She selected each one, scanned the first few lines, then moved on to the next:

Dearest Cheeryl,

I know that this must be difficult for you, so I thought that by working this out online we could recapture those old feelings. I know that this is difficult for you, but think also of how difficult this is for me?! I do really care about you, and you know that we are not just two people who met once and barely know each other. I shared so much of myself in therapy. And you too shared so much of yourself with me...

And:

> My Dear Cheeryl (Eileen Duet),
>
> How can you keep avoiding me? You know that
> our relationship can survive this, don't you? I know
> that you care about me...

One by one she read with horror the relentless expressions of
Pagnotti's frustration and repeated insistence that their 'love' could
withstand these 'difficult times.' The last messages were the most
alarming as they revealed the increasingly desperate and menacing
aspect to Pagnotti's quest to validate their 'relationship':

> Dear Eileen,
>
> I will NOT allow you to throw away our
> relationship and all that we have put into it. You
> cannot run from me. We would never have met
> face to face if fate did not intend for this to happen.
> You and I were meant for each other, and I will try
> till the day I die to be with the one I love (and the
> one who loves me in return). Don't you dare ignore
> me. Don't dare try to play with my emotions this
> way, Eileen Duet. Don't ignore your feelings for
> me and don't ignore what belongs to the both of us.

Feeling sick and her hands trembling, Eileen turned off the
computer without logging off. She left the study, climbed the
stairs and got into bed. She was exhausted, but couldn't sleep, lying
awake, heart racing, stomach turning over. Worries raced through
her mind like cars at a finish line: He had her email address, knew
where she lived, could stalk her in person or haunt her with his
messages. And if *anyone* saw the messages he sent....Oh God! What

an awful impression it would give! What a distortion of what really happened between them, she thought. But how would she ever explain what happened? How? It looked so bad. Who could she talk to? He was going to come in again next week; and again after that. He'd never stop coming. He thinks they were 'meant' to be! How sick. How sick he was! He'd never drop this...never! Someone would have to know. She would have to tell someone. But who?

She sat bolt upright and the ruminations were stricken from her mind as her ears strained to pick up what she thought was a thud downstairs. *Was it the front door? Was somebody here? Oh God, would he come back to the house?* Her body shook and her stomach was in a knot. She heard nothing. There it was again, she thought! A rustling sound. Maybe it was a tree? Would he be so crazy as to try to break into her house? Maybe he would just show up and wait outside. He was crazy! Should she call the police?

There was silence except for the wind, which was blowing hard and knocking the tree branches against the windows. She got out of bed to lock the bedroom door, avoiding the window in case he was outside looking in. Oh God, how crazy that was to think! No, no, it's not crazy—*he's* crazy! If he wanted, he could easily break the flimsy lock on the door, she thought. *And why wouldn't he come back? He's desperate.* She got back into bed and stayed silent, paralyzed by her fears.

Her body trembled through the night, but after some time she convinced herself it must be her mind playing tricks. The suicidal thoughts also helped to push away the fear. She wanted to die. She thought about how easy it would be to overdose on pills and just be done with this. Hour after hour dragged on. Throughout the night she would look at the clock, then hold her breath so she could keep as still and quiet as possible to listen for noises outside. Then she'd give up and attempt to fall back asleep. She repeated this over and over again.

He was not outside. He was terrorizing her, but he was not outside. The situation terrorized her. Her mind was terrorizing her.

It was 3 A.M., then 3:30, then 4. She tossed and turned and around 5 A.M. finally fell asleep.

Kelly was up most of the night as well, but for different reasons. Besides the fact that her twin daughters, Renee and Elise, had fevers and were coughing throughout the night, Kelly was agitated by the confrontation she had had with her sister. She wanted things to be right between them. Ron's death had devastated her too, and maybe the two of them should be consoling and supporting one another, she thought.

For the first time in her life she was feeling remorseful. This was not an emotion Kelly had any experience with. She had lived her life without either forethought or regrets; she lived only in the present. She did what felt right on that day, in that situation, in that mood, in that moment. She was living, however, with a terrible secret—a secret she believed needed to be shared, now that Eileen knew about the affair. Would there ever be a right time to discuss this with her sister? Would her sister ever be able to hear what she had to say? Could they ever restore what they had in the past?

She tossed and turned and got up several times to check on the girls. Elise was sweating and talking in her sleep. Kelly gave her more medicine and lay with her in bed for awhile. She stroked Elise's hair while her thoughts turned to Ron and how she missed him. Two hours passed when Kelly left Elise's room to check on Renee. She then returned to her own bed.

Despite having lived most of her life in a rather superficial and shallow manner, for whatever reason, Kelly now looked deep inside herself and grappled with a weighty decision. Unable to fall asleep, she went downstairs to make a cup of tea. She set her cup on the kitchen table and paced around the downstairs, unable to sit still. Several times she had the urge to phone her sister, but thought better of it. She thought about inviting her over for breakfast the next day or to visit the kids. She paced the floor and ruminated. Now that Ron was gone, she thought about unburdening herself, about sharing with her sister an important secret, which she believed could bring some closure and might possibly serve to restore their relationship.

At least she *thought* it would bring closure. Kelly often looked at things from her own perspective and considered how to relieve only *her* own unpleasant emotions. It was never about others; it was usually about herself and making herself feel better. And that was true in this case as well.

Because of Eileen's fondness for children, Kelly reasoned, maybe Renee and Elise (that is, what she needed to tell Eileen about Renee and Elise) could serve to mend her relationship with her sister. Although Eileen and Ron had agreed not to have children, the decision had not been mutual. Ron had made the choice and Eileen had grudgingly agreed, despite the fact that she loved children.

Yes, she thought, this made sense. Eileen loved kids. She loved *my* kids. *This is the right thing to do.*

She fell asleep on the couch and awoke around 7 a.m., having made up her mind to phone Eileen.

"Who is this?" a voice gravely with sleep replied.

"Eileen? It's me...Kelly."

"Kelly? You scared the hell out of me."

"I'm sorry, Eileen, is it too early? I wanted to talk to you before you went out. I really want to see you. We need to talk."

"What time is it? Why are you calling now? You really scared me," replied Eileen, the initial wave of fear subsiding as she realized it was her sister and *not* Pagnotti.

"I'm sorry. It's like seven or so. Did I wake you?" asked Kelly.

"What is it you want?" answered Eileen coldly.

"We need to talk. We can't leave this like this. I couldn't sleep all night—"

"I feel really sorry for you, Kel, not being able to get any sleep," Eileen interrupted with sarcasm.

"Eileen, come on. I'm serious. There are things we need to talk about."

"I might as well be dead, Kel. You humiliated me. You stabbed your own sister in the back—"

"Eileen, I want to talk about this face to face. I want to see you," Kelly pressed.

"I don't want to talk right now, Kelly. I just fell asleep and you scared me with the phone. Call me later. Bye."

"Wait, Eileen, Wait!" But it was too late. Eileen had hung up.

Kelly sat for a moment with the phone in her hand. She heard the kids calling so she hung up and went to check on them. Then she went to the kitchen, to get both of them a glass of juice and some toast, which she let them finish in her bedroom as they watched TV together.

Kelly, often impulsive, was about to share a secret she felt obligated to reveal, a blunder that would become one of the most painful of her life. This secret, which threatened to shatter the fragile peace she had with her family, would not mend anything; Kelly would soon learn that some secrets are best left buried. It would be a brutal transgression, though it would be accompanied by the most sincere of intentions, as are many errors in judgment.

Chapter Eleven

UNDAY MORNING WAS CRISP AND BRIGHT. THE WEATHER FORECAST had called for snow, but it was clear and beautiful as Pagnotti, yawning and stretching, rolled out of bed. The computer screen still flickered, having been left on throughout the night as usual. He got up and walked down the hallway to the bathroom where he disappeared behind a closed door.

After finishing in the bathroom—some thirty minutes later— Pagnotti returned to his room and found his father standing by, or rather stooping over and squinting at, the computer. He stopped abruptly and glared at his father for a moment—partly from shock and partly from rage—then rushed over to shut off the computer screen before turning and thrusting his face at his father, who recoiled as his son glowered at him.

"What the fuck are you doin' in here?" Pagnotti demanded to know, spitting the words into his father's face.

"I need a ride to—"

"Ya didn't come in here to ask for a ride! I'll ask again—why are ya in here?" he bellowed. His father stepped back, and Pagnotti moved forward, as if cornering his prey.

"Brock...I...uh...honestly, son, I came in here to see...to ask—" his father stammered, but before he could finish, his son shoved him back with a solid blow to his chest. Mr. Pagnotti stumbled backward, but didn't fall. "Brock, please, don't do this," he pleaded through several coughs.

"Don't do this? Don't do this?" Pagnotti repeated, mocking his father's whining pleas. "What about what you're up to, old man? Huh? What about snooping around in my room?" He backed his father up against the wall, grabbed his throat and squeezed.

"Brock...please...I...I'm having...I can't breathe!" his father rasped as his son's thumb dug into his neck. He reached up with his right hand and feebly held his son's wrist.

Then Brock threw his father to the ground and stood over him as he roared, "You're looking for dirt on me, aren't ya? Aren't ya?"

"Dirt, Brock? What are you talking about?"

"Whaddaya wanna know? What are ya looking for, ya little fuckin' snoop?" he snarled, and then he kicked his father as he lay cowering on the floor in a fetal position.

"Brock, I have no interest in what you're up to," Mr. Pagnotti insisted.

"Don't give me this bullshit! You were looking at the computer, ya little shit. What are ya lookin' for? Ya want shit on me? Is that what ya want? Ya lookin' for shit on me, old man? I'll give you some shit!"

Then he grabbed his father under the armpits, lifted him off the floor just enough to drag him down the hallway toward the bathroom. When they reached the bathroom, Mr. Pagnotti gained control of his feet and planted them squarely—though weakly—on the floor, enabling him to take a few steps. Pagnotti allowed his father to erect himself, but then continued to walk him into the bathroom.

"Brock, what are you doing? Brock?" he cried out, resisting temporarily, but his son was stronger and able to finally force him into the bathroom and down to his knees. When he had his father on his knees, he lifted the toilet seat, grabbed him by the hair on the back of his head and thrust his face into the bowl. He held it there for two or three seconds as his father's arms and legs kicked and flailed wildly.

"Ya want shit, old man? Ya want shit? I'll give ya shit! Here's the toilet, ya goddamn fool. Here's where ya get the shit!" he barked as he rhythmically threw his father's face in and out of the toilet water, cursing and threatening him.

He stopped and threw his father—chin bleeding and face soaking wet—to the bathroom floor, then wiped his hands dry on his shirt and pants. Standing triumphantly over him, Pagnotti warned, "Next time ya want some shit on me, you and I can just visit the toilet, okay? Ya just let me know, my friend, when you're getting that urge to snoop around in my room. Understood?"

Mr. Pagnotti dabbed at the blood on his chin and wiped the water from his face with his shirt sleeve, but avoiding making eye contact with his son. He sat silently.

"Understood?!" his son demanded, still standing over his father, who now lay slumped over on the bathroom floor. He pressed his knee threateningly into his father's cheek as he insisted on a response.

"Understood." Mr. Pagnotti weakly obeyed.

"I can't hear you," he son commanded.

"Understood," Mr. Pagnotti replied with a stronger voice.

Satisfied, his son turned and walked out.

The clouds thickened as the blue sky turned gray and morning gave way to early afternoon. The wind was picking up as Kelly headed toward her sister's house. Eileen remained in bed, having finally fallen asleep around nine-thirty in the morning; she had no idea her sister was on her way to further destroy whatever remained of their relationship. Kelly was determined to 'fix' things, to set things straight. She was convinced that what she had to say would make things better. Kelly's judgment, however, was far from one of her strengths. In fact, it could be counted at the top of her list of weaknesses. Nevertheless, she was on a mission now. Even her neighbor Gail was surprised that Kelly had so urgently needed to get out of the house this Sunday morning, especially with the kids not feeling well. But Gail, a stocky, sixty-one year old, never married woman with a short, thick neck and a shock of white hair was more than happy to spend some time sitting with the kids so Kelly could "spend some time with my sister."

Kelly pulled into the driveway, which was surrounded on both sides by a clutter of leaves. Eileen's house stood out among the others along her block as having the only yard without a pile of leaves neatly raked to the curb.

The shade was drawn in the window of Eileen's bedroom, but Kelly went ahead and knocked anyway. She rang the doorbell, then tried the knob, which was locked. No response. After several attempts and some ten minutes or so, Eileen's voice called from the other side, "Who is it?"

"Eileen, it's me, Kelly."

Eileen opened the door at once and stood with her arms folded across her chest, each hand clutching the opposing arm's elbow. Her eyes squinted as she adjusted to the sunlight outside. After a few moments wavering between inviting her in and slamming the door in her face, she said, "Come in, it's freezing out there."

They stood in the foyer as if the invitation was intended literally to come in from the cold but not for Kelly to venture too far inside. Eileen's body language was clear: her arms remained folded across her chest and she stood only a few steps in front of her sister, as if to corral her right where she stood. Kelly, to her credit, was not so presumptuous as to proceed any further. She didn't even attempt to remove her coat.

"Eileen, there's something I want...there's something I *need* to tell you," Kelly began, her eyes swelling with an intensity that startled her sister, who now took one step back.

"Come into the kitchen," Eileen allowed.

The two walked into the kitchen where Eileen placed a kettle
of water on the stove. Neither one spoke a word while the kettle
whistled and Eileen prepared a cup of hot water with a slice of
lemon for herself. She offered nothing to Kelly. They sat down at
the table, staring at the teacup as Eileen thoughtlessly stirred the
lemon around.

"Have you spoken to mom," asked Eileen.

"Mom? No, I haven't. I'm not sure that's necessary, is it?" asked
Kelly.

"You're unbelievable, Kelly—you know that? You really never
cease to amaze me. I now know why you can survive the way you
do. You have this knack of...of..." She stopped to her hot water, "...of
just blocking everything out so you can protect yourself, or so you
can...I don't know, maybe 'block' is not the right word, maybe *pretend*
is more appropriate. You have this knack of *pretending* that everything
is working out just as you want. You never bother with the facts. You
never let reality get in the way of what you want or how you want
things to be as long as you're happy or *your* needs are met."

"Eileen, I can't even begin to...I don't even know what I can
say to convince you that I *do* understand what you're saying. I *do*
appreciate what I've done, but I didn't come here to 'pretend' that
anything is different than it is. Or to defend myself—"

"Oh please Kel! Defend yourself? Are you serious? What do
you think I am—a fool?" Eileen interrupted, nearly dropping her
cup of hot water.

"No, no, Eileen. I'm *not* here to defend myself. Listen to what
I'm saying. I said I'm *not* defending myself. I'm here to make things
right. I need to tell you something that I think—no, that I *know*—
will make a difference for us. And I think it can bring us together.
I know it will bring us together...Eileen...I don't want to lose you
as a sister."

Eileen got up and put her cup in the sink, seemingly uninterested
in what her sister was saying. At the same time, Kelly's legs were

shaking so much she squeezed her knees together till her thighs burned under the strain.

"We need to take care of...we need to talk about caring for the kids," Kelly blurted out, a thin smile appearing as she measured Eileen's reaction.

Eileen stopped, turned, and shot a perplexed but scrutinizing look at Kelly. "What are you *talking* about?" she asked, scrunching up her nose and shaking her head.

"I want you to help me raise the kids," replied Kelly with short bursts of an uncomfortable smile. She waited for Eileen to ask for further clarification.

"What are you talking about, Kelly? What are you talking about, 'raise the kids.' You lost me."

"Eileen, you...you deserve to, you know, uhhh... to be a part of these kids' future. I-I *want* you to be a part of their future. They need to have you in their lives be...because..." she said, but she ran out of breath as she struggled to finish.

"They need to have *you*, Eileen, *you* in their lives be-cause you, Eileen..." She stopped, walked over to Eileen and took one of her hands. "Eileen, you are their father's wife, and *he* would have wanted that. I'm not sure what kind of relation that makes you," she chuckled, "but—" Then she ended instantly as she saw the expression change on her sister's face.

"He?" Eileen asked hesitatingly, though she knew who 'he' was.

"He? What do you mean, 'he'" asked Kelly naively.

"Your kids' father, Kelly? I'm his wife? 'He', Kelly, is Ron? Is that who *he* is?" asked Eileen, her speech accelerating and her voice growing louder with each word.

"Yes, Eileen, Ron is—or I should say *was* their father. This is why I thought that, well, I thought that we sort of have an ironic, well maybe ironic is not the right word—special, or maybe unique—connection."

Kelly tried to continue with her explanation of how a husband fathering the children of his wife's sister somehow bound the two sisters in some kind of divine union with important implications for the children's karma, but Eileen cut her off.

"You son of a bitch! You son of a bitch!" she wailed, as she lifted a glass from the sink and threw it to the floor, shattering it into a thousand shards. Frightened by her sister's response, Kelly stood up quickly but didn't know what to do next.

"Eileen! Eileen, take it easy," Kelly tried in an unsteady voice, though she made no attempt to move closer to Eileen, who now had smashed several plates, saucers, and small drinking glasses.

"Get out, Kelly! Get out of my house! I can't believe you would come in here to hurt me like this! Why, Kelly? Why?? What good would this do me? What, Kelly? So you can relieve your guilty conscience by coming clean on this? YOU SON OF A BITCH!" she sobbed and then with an eruption she screamed, "GET OUT!" and threw a plate across the room.

Kelly, shaken by her sister's behavior, tried no further clarifying or explaining. She hurried out the front door, got into her car and drove off, her mind playing and replaying the image of her sister's reaction—the dishes and glasses smashing on the floor, the screaming and crying. She had never in her life seen anyone so physically and violently out of control. Her hands trembled on the steering wheel and her heart pounded. She never expected this kind of response from her.

When she arrived home she sat for a moment in her driveway; then she broke down and cried.

Eileen, shocked and still standing in her kitchen, picked up a large piece of glass from the floor and walked to the bathroom where she ran the bath water. She felt numb. She was no longer crying as she removed her clothes and lowered herself into the steaming hot water. She held her right hand and arm under the running water and gingerly placed the piece of broken glass against her wrist, then pressed it against the skin. Her mind was split between what she was doing in the present moment—feeling the sharp glass against her skin—and the intense emotions she felt toward both Ron and Kelly. She was furious and she would get them all back now, she thought. She'd make her sister suffer with the guilt of having caused this suicide. The water gushed into the tub. She continued to play with the glass against her skin—to poke and cautiously stick the pointed end into her skin. She ran it delicately over the veins that stuck out on her wrist.

She thought of Pagnotti and of work, and in an instant humiliation replaced anger. How could she face anyone at work if they found out what happened with Pagnotti? She pictured herself dead in a tub filled with blood. Panic set in now and she started to cry. "Oh God, why? Why? Why?" she muttered over and over to herself as she wept.

She stopped the water and tossed the glass into the wastebasket next to the tub, then leaned back and slid down into the hot water. For some reason Michelle's face popped into mind, and Eileen wondered if she could share this with her? Could she trust her with this—not the Pagnotti situation, but the situation with her sister? She needed to talk to *someone*; she needed some kind of support. The wave of anxiety ebbed now as she decided (convinced herself) to speak to Michelle. She could not—*would* not—go through this alone. Sometimes—she recalled telling her own patients—the most important sign of strength is recognizing when you need to ask for help. Yes, a twinkle of faith seemed still to flicker inside her; she would share some of this with Michelle.

She remained in the tub awhile, calming down, at one point almost falling asleep. Eventually she got out, dried herself off and went back to the kitchen to clean up the mess she'd made. Then she went into the study to call Michelle to ask if they could meet for a cup of coffee.

"Of course I will, Eileen. Is everything okay?" asked Michelle, her soothing voice and supportive tone wrapping around Eileen like a warm blanket.

"Yes...I mean, no, not really. I need someone to talk to, Mich. Are you sure it's all right?"

"Yes of course it's all right. Now—"

"God, you have no idea how good it is to hear your voice," Eileen cut in.

"Eileen, let me pick you up, okay?" insisted Michelle. "I don't like the way you sound."

"No, Michelle, that's completely out of your way. We'll meet at the Horizon diner. Let's just meet there. I'll be fine. I just need to see you...to talk to you."

"Are you sure?" asked Michelle.

"Michelle, let's not waste the next ten minutes figuring out whether I'm sure or not sure—let's just go," answered Eileen, chuckling at her friend's characteristic over concern for her.

"All right, that's fine. I can be there in fifteen minutes."

"See you there," replied Eileen, and they hung up.

She arrived at the diner in about thirty minutes, where she saw Michelle waiting outside, leaning against the building.

"I was beginning to think you might have changed your mind," said Michelle, smiling as she gave her friend a kiss on the cheek and a hug. "You don't look well. Come on, let's go inside and get warmed up."

They walked into the nearly empty diner and waited to be seated. A short woman with a wide, overworked grin that caused her eyes to squint and a wearing uniform that looked like a garage sale bargain greeted them.

"Just the two of you?" she asked. "Smoking or non?"

"Non," answered Michelle, and at the same lime, "Smoking," said Eileen.

The waitress looked at Eileen, then at Michelle, who looked sympathetically at Eileen before turning to the waitress, "Smoking will be fine," she sighed.

The waitress walked them to their seats, handed each a menu and without pausing pulled her order pad from the front pocket of her uniform. "What can I get you folks?" she asked.

"I'll just have coffee," said Eileen right away, as she returned the menu, unopened, to the waitress.

Michelle leaned forward, "Eileen, come on, you're gonna waste away. Get something to eat."

"I'm really not hungry," Eileen insisted.

"How 'bout I come back in a bit and leave you two to decide, okay?" the waitress interjected.

"Why don't we get a tuna and split it?" offered Michelle.

"Mich, just get what you want. Get the tuna for yourself if you want it. Honestly, I'm not hungry."

Michelle relented, ordered the tuna and moved back in her chair. Her shoulders sloped, her head cocked, she smiled sympathetically at her friend, who seemed weak and frail. She reached out and held Eileen's hand, rubbing it gently while they waited for the short waitress to return.

"My God, Eileen, your hands are so cold.... I know you're going through such a tough time. It doesn't just go away in a week or a month. It's okay to feel this way, Eileen."

"That's not what I—that's not the problem, Michelle," said Eileen almost inaudibly. She looked at a napkin on the table, playing with it, folding and unfolding its corner. Michelle's face tightened as she watched her.

"What's going on, Eileen?" she asked.

"I don't know how to talk about this. This is...this is like some kind of nightmare. It feels...unreal."

"Eileen, is everything okay? What's the matter? Tell me," Michelle urged in a loud whisper, her forehead wrinkled with worry.

"You know my sister, Kelly, right?" asked Eileen after a long pause.

"Well, I think I've met her. I mean, I wouldn't know her if I saw her, but I've heard you talk about her. She lost her husband to cancer, right?"

"Six years ago."

"Okay, right." Then her eyes shot open and her mouth dropped. "That's right. Oh my God! Wow! That's unbelievable that the two of you lost your husbands," said Michelle, shaking her head.

Noticing the tears running down alongside Eileen's nose and onto her lips she exclaimed, "Oh! Eileen, I am *so* sorry. This must be so difficult for the two of you." She squeezed Eileen's hand tightly with both of hers.

"Michelle," Eileen began, once again looking at the table instead of making eye contact, "my sister was having a relationship with my husband."

Michelle's hands froze and her mouth dropped open again. Eileen glanced up for a moment to witness Michelle's expression.

"Eileen! Oh my God! Oh you poor thing!" She moved over to where Eileen sat and hugged her.

"Tuna? Should I put it over here or are you staying on this side," asked the waitress as Eileen's sobbing face was buried in Michelle's shoulder.

Michelle looked up from her embrace and replied, "Yes, just put it down there. Thank you. And the coffee goes over here."

"And you wanted a diet soda, right?" asked the waitress.

"Yes. Thank you," replied Michelle impatiently, and she returned to hugging Eileen. "Eileen, that is awful, just awful!"

In a monotone and staring down at her lap as tears fell into her hands, Eileen continued, "My sister has two daughters, Michelle," as her friend sat transfixed. "They're twins. They're twelve now—" she managed to say before her face fell into her hands and her body seemed to convulse with her sobbing.

Michelle embraced her again. "It's okay. It's okay. Just let it out. I'm here for you, Eileen. Everything's going to be okay," she said as she rubbed Eileen's back and hugged her.

Eileen gently removed herself from Michelle's firm hold and finished, "—they are Ron's kids, Michelle. My sister's kids were... fathered...by my husband. She...she told me herself."

"Oh my God! Oh my God, Eileen. I'm so sorry. I can't believe this! I am so sorry for you," Michelle repeated as tears welled up in her eyes.

They cried together for about five minutes before getting up without eating. They paid the waitress and left the diner. Without saying a word they walked together along Belmont avenue. Eileen occasionally would stop and begin sobbing. Michelle would console her, hug her and then they'd move on. They turned around after twenty minutes and walked back to the cars as it began to rain.

"Eileen, I really think you need to talk to someone," said Michelle.

"Michelle, I'll get through this," replied Eileen.

"I know you'll get through this. I'm sure you will, but I'm just worried about you. You're not right, Eileen."

"I'm not going to kill myself, if that's what you're worried about, Michelle."

"Eileen, don't talk like that. Come on, you're a therapist; you're going through a lot, and you can't do this alone. You need someone to talk to," Michelle insisted.

"You know what, Michelle. I've been going through a lot my whole life, and I'm not so sure that this is any different. And I don't really expect much to change. Some people just get dealt a bad hand. You have to learn to live with it, I guess."

Michelle shook her head at Eileen's fatalistic view, but Eileen continued, "Did I ever tell you my father was an alcoholic, Michelle?"

"Ah, that explains it," said Michelle. "An adult child of an alcoholic. An A-C-O-A—"

"Oh stop, Michelle. Stop with the labels and the jargon," said Eileen, cutting her off. "Please don't analyze me. I'm simply pointing out that, for whatever reason, I've really had a hard life, and it's like...it's like, I don't know...like I've got some black cloud hanging over me—"

"Eileen, don't talk like that. You don't have a black cloud over you. You grew up with an alcoholic dad and that's horrible; and you know how that can affect a person later on in life," Michelle asserted, looking her friend directly in the eyes. "You've been making excuses your whole life for other people's faults, Eileen. You've tried to make everyone's life just right, even if it meant you had to suffer. This wasn't your fault, Eileen. This doesn't mean you have a black cloud over you, but you do need to get help."

"You know what, Michelle? I appreciate being able to talk to you. I really do—"

"Eileen, this is not enough. I am *not* your therapist. You need to talk to somebody."

"Okay, okay, okay. I'm going to do something about this. I will. I promise. Look, I really appreciate your taking time to meet and talk with me; I really do. I know I can count on you and that's important. I really appreciate it, but you know what? I'm tired now and I think I need to just get home and get some rest," she said as she hugged Michelle.

"Are you going in tomorrow?" asked Michelle.

"I don't know. What do you think? I mean, are you thinking I should take more time off?" replied Eileen.

"I think you need to keep busy, Eileen. You can't sit home and stew about this stuff. You need to be around people."

"I don't know. Maybe I'll be in."

"If you don't come in, I'm gonna call you, okay? I wanna make sure you're doing okay? All right?" Michelle insisted.

"Fine. I'll call you if I don't go in tomorrow. But I want you to stop worrying about me. Everything's going to be okay.... And thanks again, Michelle, really. Thank you. This means a lot to me."

"Anything you need, just ask." offered Michelle as they parted with a kiss and one final hug.

Eileen got into her car and drove off just as the rainfall turned heavy. What had started out as a beautiful, clear morning had turned gray and wet. There was no way she would go in tomorrow, she decided. She usually saw Pagnotti on Mondays, but she couldn't face him tomorrow—not this soon. She had to face him some time; that was true. But it didn't have to be tomorrow; tomorrow just wasn't the right time. She'd call in sick, she planned, and they'd have to reschedule him. If all worked out right, she could buy at least a week's time before he'd be back.

Lost in her thoughts, Eileen nearly hit a car as she pulled away from a stop sign. The car honked loudly, and the driver shot her a rude gesture, but she hardly noticed. Maybe, she thought, she'd be better off if some car smashed into hers and killed her. Then she wouldn't have to deal with Pagnotti, or with her sister. She put the thoughts out of her mind, turned the radio up loud and somehow found her way home.

When she got into the house, she went up to her room, changed her clothes and got into bed. She slept straight through to the next morning. Around nine-fifteen she called in sick to work. She rolled over and went back to sleep. Her Monday was just beginning. She'd avoid Pagnotti for the moment—in session, at least—but wouldn't avoid him altogether.

Chapter Twelve

T HE PHONE RANG AROUND NOON, STARTLING EILEEN FROM HER sleep and provoking a wave of panic. Three deep breaths and two rings later she fumbled for the phone, dropped it once, then brought it to her ear, "H-h-hello? Who is this?" she asked tensely.

"I'm so sorry, did I wake you, Eileen?" asked Mary.

"Mary?"

"Yes."

"No, that's okay. I, uh, I just got scared, you know, when the phone wakes you up. Is everything all right?"

"Well, I just thought you should know this," Mary began. "Mr. Pagnotti was here because we weren't able to reach him at home to cancel his appointment. And...well...he was really making a scene here—"

"What did he say, Mary?" Eileen exclaimed in a loud voice.

"Oh, see, I knew you'd want to know this. You know, the guy's really a little weird, but this was really crazy even for him. And I knew you wouldn't mind if I—"

"Mary, please!" Eileen pleaded. "Just tell me what happened!"

"I'm sorry! Okay, well...he was just...he was yelling and telling us we were full of you-know-what, and he insisted on seeing you—"

"Did he say anything else, Mary? Anything? What else did he say?" Eileen begged.

"Eileen, relax. I'm telling you what he said. That's what he said. He was just yelling—"

"What exactly was he saying when he was yelling. I know he was yelling, but what was he saying?"

"Eileen, *please* don't yell at me. I had enough yelling this morning."

"I'm sorry, Mary, really I am. I don't mean to yell at you. I-I-I'm just not myself. I'm not feeling well," she explained. She squeezed the phone, got out of bed and began to pace as she continued, "It's not your fault, really, I-I'm really sorry, Mary."

"Well, the only reason I'm bothering you at home is that he was insisting on rescheduling his appointment this week. He wouldn't leave and he was saying he was going to complain and write to his insurance company and all that. So the only thing I could do was to fit him into your lunchtime for tomorrow. I hope that's all right," Mary said, her voice rising apologetically. "I didn't want you to come in here tomorrow and think I just made some mistake. I really needed to do something and I didn't know what, so I just wanted you to know. You think that was okay?" And in a hushed voice she added, "He's really weird, you know?"

"I know, I know, Mary. It's okay. You did the right thing. You did the right thing. I really appreciate you calling me to let me know. Really—thank you." And she was thankful, but her stomach churned.

They hung up and Eileen lay back in her bed and stared at the ceiling. How could she face him, she wondered. And how long before he started blackmailing her with information about what happened between them? Over and over she obsessed. Agitated and unable to fall back to sleep, she got up and started to shower.

After finishing in the shower and wrapping herself in a towel, she thought she heard a thudding sound and then rustling downstairs, so she walked over to the window to check on the weather. It must be the wind picking up, she thought. The sky was overcast, but the trees were still. A gray Nissan Sentra sat parked in front of the house, the back end of the car partially blocking her driveway.

She turned away from the window, drying her hair with a second towel, when again she thought she heard something downstairs. This time she was certain it was not the wind. Her heart quickened even before she was aware that what she thought she heard were...footsteps? She stopped abruptly and held her breath, listening intently. *It can't be.* No—that's ridiculous, she thought. But there it was again! Someone was walking downstairs, she was sure! She tiptoed to her bedroom door and listened again. There was silence. She walked out of her room and moved quietly to the top of the stairs. She paused, then descended two steps and froze. There he was. Brock Pagnotti was standing in her house!

His mouth broke into a sinister grin, hers dropped open and her eyes bulged. They continued staring at each other until Eileen finally managed to utter, "Oh my God! My God!" Her skin crawled, her limbs stiffened, and she began to hyperventilate after what felt like an injection of adrenaline.

"Goin' somewhere? I thought maybe we could make up our missed session here," he said menacingly, then he bounded up the stairs two at a time.

Stunned by the suddenness of what happened, Eileen felt stuck, as if in a nightmare where no matter how hard you try you're legs just won't budge. Finally she turned, dashed to her room and attempted to close the door in front of him; but he was too quick. He held the door open as she pulled back with all her strength. "No! No! Go away!" she wailed over and over again as she struggled in vain to shut the door.

Her arms quivering as she squeezed the doorknob and strained to pull it closed, Eileen finally reached exhaustion and the door flung open, smashing against the wall. She stumbled backwards a couple of steps but maintained her balance as she stared in horror at him standing in her bedroom violating whatever boundaries remained in their warped relationship. The grin on his face melted into a leer as his eyes slithered up and down her body. It was this look that instantly reminded her that she was standing before him dripping wet in just a towel. Her hands held tightly to the towel as she stepped backwards.

"Brock, what is it you want? Brock, think about what you're doing. Can you please get out of my house, and we can talk about this?" Eileen implored, her voice trembling with fear. It was then that she noticed the knife in his hand. She hadn't noticed it initially, but he was now wagging it threateningly at his waist.

"I *know* what I want, Eileen. I'm looking at what I want and it's lookin' mighty nice, if I do say so. Yep, you are lookin' very nice—"

"PLEASE, Brock! You don't want to do this!" she begged, her voice screeching as its volume rose.

"Why didn't you come in today? You gonna take off every day you're supposed to see me?" he asked, still waving the knife at his side.

"No, Brock, that's not—"

"You can't avoid me forever, ya' know."

"I'm not avoiding you, Brock. But this is not the way to discuss this. You don't belong in here." She stepped back again, her fingers fumbling at the towel to ensure she was covered.

"DON'T TELL ME WHERE I BELONG AND DON'T BELONG!" he bellowed, as she took another step backward; he followed forward. "We had something special, and you know it," he continued. "We had chemistry, Eileen. You wanna just blow me off like my feelings don't count!"

Pagnotti had now backed her up against the foot of her bed. He held the knife out, holding it upright, twirling it not more than four or five inches from her nose.

"B-Brock, please...please put the knife away. Let's take a moment to think about this. I-I want you to think about what you're doing, Brock," she managed to say, her knees weakening and then buckling momentarily as the stiffness in her muscles was reaching its limit.

"Oh, yeah, let's think about it. Let's think about my anger, right? Maybe I can identify the trigger and try to change my *'cognitions'* right, Doc? Am I going to owe you anything for this session?" Pagnotti chuckled mockingly.

He reached out with his free hand and tried to brush her cheek with the back of his fingertips, but she snapped her head away. Instantly her eyes shot back at his, as she realized her reflexive rebuff of his advance was exactly the wrong move, converting his lighthearted tone to fury. He grabbed a handful of her hair and pulled her face forward towards his.

"You're a fuckin' little princess, aren't ya? You bitch! YOU BITCH!" he boomed with his stinking breath, his lips nearly brushing against her nose. "You're too good for me, right? But ya weren't too good for me when ya were crying online about your husband hurtin' ya, were ya?" He tugged her hair again and brought the tip of the steely blade up to her nose. "Ya wanted me then, ya bitch, didn't ya? DIDN'T YOU?" he roared.

"P-p-please, s-s-stop, Brock. P-p-please d-don't hurt me, please. I'll d-d-d-o anything for you. J-j-just don't—"

"WHAT'S IT GONNA BE, EILEEN? WHAT?" he demanded.

"W-w-what, Brock? What do you want? I-I-I don't know what you're asking," Eileen appealed.

He pushed her to the bed and inexplicably turned his back on her, taking a few steps away—a reprieve, she thought. Her heart jumped for a moment as she thought it might be over, that he might be leaving.

"I wanna know what it's gonna be for us, Eileen?" he asked in a starkly different—softer—tone.

"For us?" she repeated quietly, sitting up cautiously on the bed like his prey, moving gently to avoid drawing his attention or provoking an attack. Her eyes remained riveted on him as he seemed to strut about her room. "Brock...there...we can't..." Then her voice changed, strengthened by confidence as she sensed his retreat, "Brock, this is not the way to discuss this. You're right, though; we do need to discuss 'us,'" she offered deceitfully in an attempt to join his deluded perspective and soften his predatory stance.

He turned and looked suspiciously at her from the sides of his eyes. Then he walked to her dresser and began tinkering with a number of figurines and pictures. Without looking back at her, he walked to the doorway, pressed the tip of the knife into the wall and scratched a line downward on the paint. Then he punched the wall, causing her to jump. "Fuck you, you whore!" he growled in frustration. He snapped the knife shut, turned and said, "This isn't over, babe." The use of 'babe' sent a shiver down her spine. "I'm not here to hurt ya. I'm just here to have what belongs to me; that's all. I'm not gonna let ya play with my feelings." Then the sinister smile reappeared. "You're my therapist, hun. You should know better than to play with a man's feelings."

He walked out with a loud guffaw. She heard him clumsily descend the steps and let himself out. She dashed to the window and watched as he got into his car and drove off, after which she collapsed onto the bed and cried uncontrollably, her heart beating so wildly she thought it might burst.

He came into my house and could have raped me! He held a knife to my face! Maybe she could go to the police now. Was that the answer? No way. They were sure to discover she had chatted online with him and had met him in person. *This can never come out. Never!* These details were far too humiliating and scandalous to allow others to know. Her career would be over, she fretted. "Oh God! How could I have gotten into this mess!" she cried.

Her stomach in a knot, the anxiety unrelenting, suicide seemed more and more like the answer, the way out, the chance to turn the pain off and end the suffering. When they first occurred, the suicidal thoughts scared her; now they were comforting. Even if only for a moment, the abrupt cessation of anxiety was stunning in its completeness. She never before thought of anxiety as pain, but that's exactly what it was—it hurt and it hurt badly. Her body ached and had ached for quite awhile. But when she visualized her dead body being discovered—*by the police? by Kelly? by Michelle?*—she immediately experienced a break, as if suddenly going deaf in the midst of rush hour in Manhattan. It was peace; it was silence. Suicide was an answer...an answer to all her problems, she thought. It could all be over; it *would* all be over. This fantasy felt so good to revel in, but it was a bliss whose intensity lay simply in its contrast to the surrounding emotional anguish. It wasn't really a solution at all.

Once again, however, she considered cutting her wrist. She pictured specifically what she'd use (*the sharp blade on the orange box cutter she kept in the drawer next to the utensils*). Or it may be easier, she thought, to overdose on pills (*Tylenol, Advil?*) with the help of as much liquor as she could tolerate. Or maybe it was easiest simply to park the car in the garage, run the engine, and end it peacefully. *Don't you just fall asleep?* On and on she mulled over her options, which kept out the shame-filled thoughts and guilt. No longer focused on her problems, she was fixated on a final solution as she gradually slipped back into a deep sleep.

The ringing shook her from her sleep. She sat up on her elbows, her eyes transfixed on the phone. Was he calling her? It rang again. Oh my God! This is unbelievable, she thought, as the pain and anxiety returned in all its ferocity. It rang a third time, but her body just trembled—she was frozen. After the fourth ring, the answering machine picked up:

"Hi Eileen, it's Michelle. I'm just calling—"

Eileen's trance broke immediately and she grabbed for the phone, blurting out, "Michelle! I'm here!"

"Well, I should hope you're there," chuckled Michelle. "What are you doing, screening your calls? I guess I should consider myself privileged that you picked up for me."

"Oh, Michelle, I'm so glad it's you?" replied Eileen, exhaling as if she had just sprinted up the stairs.

"Who did you think it was? Who are you avoiding?" Michelle asked lightheartedly.

"No one...I-I'm just glad...Hey, what time is it?"

"Eileen, are you in bed? Did I wake you?"

"No. I mean...I mean sort of. I was just taking a nap," she lied.

"It's about five-fifteen. I was just about to leave and I hadn't heard from you. I was checking in on you. How are you?"

"Uh...well, I'm good. I'm good, Michelle. I'm glad I took the day off," replied Eileen.

"Valerie is retiring. Do you know her?" Michelle continued.

"Valerie? I'm not sure I know her."

"Valerie, the one from downstairs. The one who ran that group for adolescent girls last year, remember?"

"Oh, yeah, maybe. I think so. So she's retiring?"

"They're collecting money for a goodbye luncheon."

"Luncheon? For who?" replied Eileen after a brief pause.

"Valerie. I just said Valerie is retiring, Eileen."

"Right, right, I heard you. I'm...I'm just...I'm just out of it, I guess," replied Eileen with a feigned laugh. "Anything else new there? Did I miss anything?" she asked.

They chatted about various goings-on at the office, discussed a few rumors, and carried on for some time with small talk before Michelle offered, "Do you want me to stop and bring you something for dinner? Tim is not coming home till late because—"

"Stop here? No! No, Michelle, don't stop here," Eileen insisted, her voice betraying her agitation.

Baffled by Eileen's tone and distractibility but not wanting to pressure her friend, Michelle refrained from digging further (as was her wont). Instead, she responded, "Okay, no problem. That's fine. You sure you don't want something or me to just stop by? Is there anything I can do?"

After a pause, "No, that's nice of you to ask, Michelle. I do appreciate it," said Eileen, trying her best to sound matter-of-fact. "I don't need anything. I *am* going to be in tomorrow. I'm fine, really."

"All right. I know, you're a tough one, Eileen." And the two exchanged contrived laughs. "I guess I'll see you tomorrow then, right?"

"Yep, I'll be in tomorrow. Maybe we'll do lunch, okay Mich?"

"Okay, that sounds good—"

"NO! Forget that. That's no good," said Eileen, abruptly cutting off Michelle in mid-sentence as she realized her lunch hour would be used for Pagnotti. Whatever respite Michelle had provided with her cheery, unconcerned and lighthearted banter had been obliterated by the reality that tomorrow she was to face Pagnotti again. It just didn't go away! It would never go away, she dreaded.

"Eileen?"

"Yes? I'm sorry, Mich. I'm sorry. Look, forget lunch tomorrow. I had to have a patient rescheduled there...I'm sure we'll see each other. Maybe the next day we'll do lunch or catch up with each other, okay?"

"That's fine, Eileen. Just take care of yourself, all right?"

"I will. I will. Thanks, Mich....Okay, well, I'll see you tomorrow."

They hung up, Eileen falling flat on her back onto the bed, staring at the ceiling; Michelle staring, still mystified, at the phone, replaying in her mind the odd conversation she had with Eileen.

Eileen finally got up and dressed, but then spent time looking through the medicine cabinet. She was planning, figuring things out, but not intending anything just yet. She left her bedroom and went downstairs to lock her front door.

Chapter Thirteen

T HE NEXT MORNING WAS BITTER COLD. EILEEN CRAWLED OUT OF bed slowly, walked to the window and pressed her fingers against the frozen glass. She had remained in bed through the previous day and spent most of the night tossing, turning and dreading this morning's scheduled appointment with Pagnotti. The anxiety returned as a queasy feeling emerged in her stomach and left her feeling nauseous. She pressed her cheek against the window; her eyes squeezed tightly shut as she fought back against Pagnotti's image in her mind. "What did I do? How stupid! How stupid I was!" she cried out as she gently banged the window with a fist.

She went to the bathroom to brush her hair and teeth, but neglected her teeth as she decided out of curiosity to step on the scale. She was continuing to lose weight, which concerned her momentarily, only to be pushed aside by the horrifying image of Pagnotti's loathsome grinning face that had haunted her throughout the night. The more she tried not to think about him, the more vivid was the image.

After leaving the bathroom and getting dressed, she walked out of her room, keeping her eyes—as best she could—averted from the knife mark Pagnotti had left on the wall the day before. It was a deep gash where he had first stabbed the wall angrily, but the mark gradually faded into just a scratch about six inches down. The thought *My throat* came to mind, but she hurried out of the room and out the front door before allowing it to finish.

She arrived at the clinic parking lot, the wind blowing hard as she got out of her car; she wrapped her scarf tightly around her neck and clutched her coat closed as she walked briskly to the building. She was greeted by what seemed like an unusually warm reception, though it seemed that since her husband had died she was constantly the recipient of sorrowful expressions and sympathetic remarks and gestures. She hated being the object of everyone's pity, or thinking she was a popular topic of water cooler conversations. Although she didn't realize, it was guilt over what she was hiding and not how the staff behaved that stirred her feelings of paranoia.

As she passed Jeremy in the hallway, she declined—with one word—his offer to buy her a cup of coffee from the cafeteria, preferring instead to head straight to her office. She retrieved her phone messages without a word to any of the support staff and then scurried to her room and closed herself in. No sooner had she begun to sort through her mail than the phone rang announcing a new patient she had to evaluate. "Thanks, Mary, I'll be there in a sec. Just ask them to wait," she said. Seeing patients was a sure way to distract her thoughts, but with each new patient, she felt the noon hour—and Pagnotti—hurtling closer and closer.

Around twenty minutes past the hour, Eileen emerged from her office to introduce herself to the new patient. The patient angrily complained about having to wait, but Eileen reassured her she would be able to get her out on time. She did not. Each patient that followed ran later than the previous one, so that by noon she was only beginning with her eleven-fifteen appointment. Eileen's anxiety rose precipitously, as the clock read twelve-ten. Distracted by each passing minute, she could barely follow her patient's story, wondering why Mary had not yet called to announce Pagnotti's arrival.

"Eileen?" she heard her patient call out, her head shifting quickly to meet her eyes.

"Yes? Jackie...you were saying—" said Eileen.

"Are you listening to what I'm saying?" asked her patient, a diminutive woman with a chronic depression.

"Of course I am...You were saying that—Oh my God!" Eileen shrieked, clutching the arms of her chair as both she and her patient jerked their heads toward the knocking at the door.

"Oops, I'm so sorry, Ms. Duet. Pardon me," Helen, from housekeeping, apologized, quickly ducking out and shutting the door behind her.

Eileen held her hand to her chest and breathed heavily. Looking up at Jackie's wide-eyed expression, she gave a nervous laugh and offered, "Well, that certainly was startling, wasn't it?"

"You...you don't seem like yourself, Eileen....You really seem on edge today."

Eileen dismissed her patient's observations and struggled to continue with the session, but she couldn't shake Pagnotti from her mind. Her forehead throbbed under the strain of her squinting eyes darting from her patient to the clock and back to her patient. Pagnotti was never late. He never missed a session; and after the scene he created in the office yesterday, insisting on a makeup, his absence now at twelve-twenty was utterly extraordinary.

"Did you hear what I said?" asked Jackie timidly, startling Eileen out of her preoccupation.

"I'm sorry?" replied Eileen, taking a second to find her focus and then the patient's eyes.

"I was saying that—" Jackie started but then paused, looking curiously at Eileen. Are you okay? You still seem distracted."

"I'm sorry. No, I'm fine. You were saying something about your husband, right?" said Eileen, attempting to recover once again.

"No, not my *husband,* my *daughter.* I wanted to know if it would be all right to bring my daughter to our next meeting," replied Jackie, sounding rather vexed.

Eileen apologized and did her best to bring closure to the session without seeming completely incompetent. The patient left without scheduling a follow-up, telling Eileen she didn't have her date book and would have to call when she returned to work. This excuse only served to further embarrass her as she felt she was letting her patients down. It also made clear how badly she was allowing her preoccupation and personal problems to impair her work. How long could this go on, she worried.

By twelve-thirty Eileen had called Mary three times to ask if Pagnotti arrived. "Why don't you just go to lunch and I'll tell him his appointment was for noon," suggested Mary.

"Oh God, no, Mary! You saw how he acted yesterday. I'd have to at least wait till one," replied Eileen.

"Ah, I think you need to be tough with guys like this, Eileen," Mary teased. "What are you going to do if he shows at five to one?"

"Good question. I guess I'd see him for five minutes and have him reschedule for next week. That's being tough, isn't it?" said Eileen with a chuckle.

"Well, it's like twenty-five or twenty to one. I really don't think he's coming. It always happens when someone insists on having a certain appointment. The more they argue and insist and have their little tantrum, the less likely they are to actually keep the appointment. At least that's what I think," said Mary with the air of confidence that secretaries have when given the opportunity to share the wisdom they glean from their positions at the hub of a "At least that's what I think," said Mary, her tone reflecting the insights she had gained from her unique position within the clinic.

"I know. I know, that's so true, Mary; you're right. But this is really, really strange for him. I don't think he's ever missed a session. And if he's not ten minutes early, that's considered late for him....All right, well, I'll be here if he does show."

He never did show. Eileen's day dragged on with patient after patient whose faces seemed to blend together and whose stories fell onto either deaf or unsympathetic ears. The longer the day went, the more she wondered what happened to Pagnotti. When the day ended, she was faced with a difficult decision. Should she call him to find out why he missed his session and then document her attempt in a progress note as she would any other high risk patient? The thought of having to call this person who had just begun to... terrorize? Yes! Terrorize is the right word. How could she reach out to this despicable monster? The thought appalled her. *But it's all my fault!* she agonized.

She eventually managed to place the call, letting it ring three times. After the third ring, she quickly hung up and wrote a progress note detailing his 'no show' and her attempt to reach him. Then she left for the night.

Her mind never stopped racing from the moment she left until she arrived home. Was he waiting at her home to have his session there? What a perverse thought, but it *was* possible! He *could* come back! She arrived to an empty house with no cars in sight and nothing unusual about the house. She hesitated at the doorstep and looked around to be extra sure, scanning the area by the garage, the windows...even the roof. She walked into the empty and silent house, quickly locking the door behind her and wondering how long she could go on like this—jumping at every shadow, gasping at every sound, and panicking at every phone call.

The weather over the next several days was unseasonably warm. The sun shone brightly and the ground began to soften under the thaw. Despite the rising temperatures, Eileen felt cold every day. Her body weakened as her appetite continued to decline; she rarely ate, and when she did she was forcing merely soup or a cracker or two. She had worked the past several days constantly on guard: looking over her shoulder and walking hastily wherever she went; dashing from her house to her car, and from her car to the clinic. And on her return home, she did the same in reverse—running from clinic to car and from car to house, locking all doors immediately.

She wondered whether Pagnotti was playing some kind of cruel joke on her. He hadn't shown for his last appointment—the only appointment he'd ever missed—and he hadn't called to reschedule. She had left two messages for him, but heard nothing back. Not knowing where he was or what he was up to was torturous. Would he just pop up one day at her house? Or at work? Would he be waiting by her car? What was he up to, she wondered. Her anxiety rose and her functioning further eroded with each passing day, until Friday when the detective called.

"Eileen, there's a detective—*Thanger* or *Tanger* I think—on the phone for you," said Mary, her hushed voice conveying a sense of intrigue.

"A detective? Wanting to talk to *me*?" Eileen was puzzled. "Well go ahead and put him through."

After a moment to transfer the call, a gentle but deep, gravelly voice announced: "Eileen Duet, this is Detective Sanger."

"Detective Sanger?" Eileen repeated.

"Yes. I'm calling you because I understand you were a therapist for a Mr. Brock Pagnotti. Is that right?"

Her body shuddered with the mentioning of his name. Her immediate thought was that she was in trouble. She had been found out! *Is it true? This was crazy.* Was she in trouble for meeting him? She'd have to come up with an excuse. *It wasn't intentional!* It was all a mistake, the voice in her head shouted. She would explain everything—the chatting (*It was anonymous! I really didn't know I was chatting with HIM!*), and mistakenly agreeing to meet him when she really didn't know who she was meeting. She'd have to explain it all!

Should I have told someone? They'll want to know why I didn't tell anyone or go to the police. Why didn't I go to my supervisor? Why didn't I explain the mistake right away? Why didn't I remove myself as his therapist? On and on her mind raced. She was speechless.

"Ms. Duet? You still there?" said the detective, interrupting her confused silence.

"Yes...Yes, I'm here," she answered.

"If you're wondering about consent or permission to speak to me, forget it. I'm calling because Mr. Pagnotti was found dead. It looks like a suicide. His father called—"

"Pagnotti is dead?" Eileen erupted. "Did you say...what happened?" she blurted out. She didn't know if she should burst into cheer or simply thank the detective. She did neither; she remained in control, her anxiety evaporated as the detective's resonating voice repeated his pronouncement: Pagnotti was dead. She was elated!

"He was found with a bullet to his head. He didn't leave a note, but his father says his son had mental problems," explained the detective. "The father gave us your number. He's the one who found him. Seems this Brock guy—the mental one—he was dead a couple of days, but his father—a nice guy, I might add—was afraid to knock on his bedroom door or disturb him. Says his son was unstable and if the father did the wrong thing his son might lose it. But after a couple of days he just decided to go on into his son's room to see what was going on, and there he was lying on the floor with his head in a pool of blood. Sounds like a real nut, if you don't mind me saying."

"I cannot believe this. I really can't believe this," Eileen muttered, still stunned by the news.

"Was he talkin' about offin' himself, Ms. Duet? Ever talk about stuff like that with you?" asked the detective.

"No. I mean...well yes...occasionally. Not recently. I mean, in the past he made lot's of threats, but he was one of those patients who always talked about killing himself—always making threats, but never acted on it," explained Eileen, her face beaming with excitement.

"When was the last time you saw him, Ms. Duet?" Detective Sanger continued matter-of-factly.

"I'm not sure. Actually, he was supposed to be here on Monday—no, Tuesday. I was out on Monday when I was originally supposed to see him," she said quickly, nearly tripping over her words. "Then he was rescheduled for Tuesday, but he didn't show to that appointment. It was unusual because he almost never missed a session. He was always consistent—to a fault. So the last time I saw him—"

She stopped abruptly, choking on her words. The image of Pagnotti in her house on Monday flashed through her mind. She saw him vividly in her mind's eye holding the knife to her face, yelling at her, calling her 'babe,' trying to stroke her face, promising—*threatening*—that "this isn't over." *That* was really the last time she saw him. His horrid face and those baleful eyes swelled in her mind, evoking a wave of panic that cut through her stomach, making her double over in pain.

Should she tell the detective about that incident? *Wouldn't that just complicate matters unnecessarily? Did anyone need to know what happened, now that he was dead?* If she mentioned *any* of that, it would be so confusing she would end up having to explain it *all.* How could she possibly tell the detective that Pagnotti broke into her house, but she didn't call the police? The whole story would *have* to come out if she mentioned this. It just didn't make sense. None of it made sense!

There was silence while questions clogged her mind.

"Ms. Duet? You were saying?" the detective spoke up.

"Yes. I'm sorry."

"When was the last time you saw him?" the detective asked again.

"I didn't see him this week, so it was probably a week ago Monday. Yes, it was a week ago Monday," she answered.

"And he wasn't talking about killing himself then, Ms. Duet?"

"No. No he wasn't. That doesn't mean he wasn't suicidal. But when he was asked, he denied it."

"And you asked him that day, Ms. Duet?" the detective persisted, trying to clarify her answer.

"I asked him every session, Detective Sanger, Eileen asserted defensively.

"I'm just asking because I need to have all this information. Of course, there'll be an autopsy too. That's standard. But for the medical examiner to declare a cause of death, all this information is going to be helpful. If you ask me, though, I'd tell ya' this guy went bonkers and blew his brains out. But you guys are the professionals, not me," the detective chuckled.

"Is there anything else you need, detective?" asked Eileen, one hand squeezing the phone, the other holding her stomach.

"Nah, nothing now, but I may be in touch. Thanks a lot, Ms. Duet. You have a nice day."

They hung up and Eileen sat frozen for several minutes. She'd normally be distraught over the loss of one of her patients; instead she was overwhelmed by this turn of events. In fact, her feelings were rather mixed. She hadn't seen this coming. Pagnotti was always making threats that he didn't follow through on. And truthfully, she hadn't routinely asked him about suicide over the last several sessions, despite what she told the detective.

Nevertheless, there was no doubt this was welcome news. She no longer had to live in fear of the consequences of her poor judgment. She no longer had to fear his email, or his threatening her, or showing up at her house! Pagnotti was gone, and she could now start putting her life back together again; she could put this behind her.

Or so she thought.

Chapter Fourteen

ILEEN'S APPETITE INCREASED THROUGHOUT THE WEEKEND. SHE hadn't made herself a full meal, but she at least was eating fairly large salads with some tuna or chicken. She had cleaned her closets and had tidied up the house after weeks of neglect. She returned to work on Monday in much better spirits despite the light snow that was falling and the slick roadways, which had extended her short commute to twenty minutes.

When Eileen arrived on her floor, Dr. Diane Thomas, the supervisor, invited her into her office so they could speak alone.

"Please sit down," Dr. Thomas suggested. "We need to fill out some paperwork for the Clinical Review Committee."

"Clinical Review Committee?" asked Eileen.

"The Review Committee reviews all untoward events: unanticipated deaths, suicide attempts, and completed suicides. You'll have to present Pagnotti's case to the committee," explained Dr. Thomas.

Eileen became uneasy, shifting in her seat and crossing her legs. "Present the case?" she asked.

"It's not a big deal," Dr. Thomas began with a sympathetic smile. "I know this is a difficult time for you. It's always hard when you lose one of your patients. But the committee has time constraints, and they need information for both their own quality control and for the insurance company."

"I see," Eileen muttered, her knitted brow betraying her concern.

"I know you were seeing Pagnotti a lot, and I know he was a difficult case. And I also know how hard you worked at managing the risk he constantly presented to you. This is really just routine, so you can wipe that worried look off your face." And after a pause, she added, "Are you okay?" as she strained her neck down and forward attempting to meet Eileen's eyes.

"Yes. Yes, I'm okay. You know, when he didn't show last week I made several calls and documented all of that. He wasn't talking about suicide the last times I saw him, Diane," Eileen began defensively.

"I know. I know. Just tell me when you last saw him, and I'll need for you to get me his medical record number. I'll fill out the top part of this form, and then I'll let you put in the other info, like what the detective said and where and how they found his body, okay?" explained Dr. Thomas, her voice gentle with sympathy as she handed Eileen the form.

"That's no problem. I just need to get the chart, though."

"Right, that's fine. You don't have to do this here. But I do need this done this morning so I can fax it over to them," replied Dr. Thomas.

"And when do I have to meet with the committee?" asked Eileen.

"It'll probably be early next week. I'd also like you to present the information to the staff. I know they've heard you present his case many times before, but we're also expected to do some kind of staffing of the case, okay? And then Dr. Levinson, the medical director, will review the chart. He heads the review committee. He'll explain all this to you at the meeting; he's a great guy, really."

Eileen nodded and stood up to leave. Dr. Thomas stood up quickly and looked her in the eyes. "Eileen, how are you doing, really?" she asked as she reached out gently grasping Eileen's wrist.

"I'm fine, really," Eileen replied impassively.

"If you want to take some time off, that would be okay, you know?" offered Dr. Thomas.

"No, no, I don't need any more time off. Besides, I think seeing patients and just keeping busy will help keep this off my mind," replied Eileen.

"Well, you let me know, okay?"

"I will," said Eileen, and she turned and walked out.

Eileen pulled the chart immediately after leaving Dr. Thomas's office, eager to scour the record for any signs she may have mishandled the case. She was certain her work as reflected in the record would be unremarkable. She had documented every conversation she had with him and documented every time she presented the case to the staff. She had tried to outreach him when he didn't show last Monday, and she documented that he had denied suicidal ideation or intent or plans whenever that was true. And when he hinted at suicidal thoughts, she had him hauled over to the emergency room.

She was sure the record would be impeccable; still, the secret she held about their encounters and her inadvertent chatting with him troubled her. She was reassured by reminding herself that no one else knew anything about what she did...no one but him, she thought. And Pagnotti was no longer around to tell.

Eileen was correct to assume that seeing patients would take her mind off her eventual meeting with the Review Committee—that, and the fact that her own review of the Pagnotti record turned up nothing remarkable. There were no gaps, she presented the case frequently to the staff for assistance, and every phone call was documented in detail, as was every assessment of his suicide risk. She felt confident and unworried as the meeting approached.

Life was slowly returning to normal for Eileen. She saw patients, ate regularly, slept soundly, and she fell into most of her old routines both at home and at the office. All had seemed ordinary at work until that Friday when Dr. Thomas called Eileen in for another meeting. This time, Dr. Thomas's demeanor offered none of the compassion and kindness of their previous meeting. She was stiff, formal, and offered little eye contact.

The door shut loudly behind them, and Dr. Thomas offered Eileen a seat. It was hard to tell, but it seemed as though anger underlay Dr. Thomas's tense expression. Or maybe she was just concerned or upset but not angry. But about what, Eileen wondered.

"I'm not quite sure how to speak to you about this, Eileen," Dr. Thomas began. She rubbed her palms several times along her thighs toward her knees, her arms rigid.

"Is something wrong, Diane?" Eileen asked barely managing to push the words out of her tightening throat and dry mouth.

Dr. Thomas's breathing could be heard as she sighed loudly through her nostrils, her lips pressed tightly together. "Eileen... you were under quite a bit of stress when you returned from your leave—after your husband's death, that is," stated Dr. Thomas.

Eileen's pulse raced. Where is she headed with this, she wondered. "I'm okay, Diane. I'm not following you. I took time off and I returned when I was ready. And that was quite awhile ago. What's going on?"

"Yes, okay, this is confusing. Let me say it this way. Let me just be up front with you about my concern," Dr. Thomas replied, shifting in her seat and clasping her fingers together. "I'm very concerned about some things that may have been happening to you in your personal life after that loss that...well...that may have affected you in a way that made it difficult—emotionally—for to do your job. And I'm wondering how much that may have played a role in what happened with Pagnotti."

"Diane, are you blaming me for Pagnotti's suicide?" Eileen protested, her voice rising with indignation.

"Eileen, no, of course not! Please, let me finish because I haven't said what I have to say. This isn't about blame. I'm trying to figure something out; that's all. And I have a right to figure this out. This is my job. I need to know if a therapist of mine whose patient committed suicide was in a state of mind that would allow her to do her job—that's all. My supervision of you—of any of my staff— can be questioned if I allow any of you to practice when there's a problem going on, or you're impaired in some way—"

"Impaired? Diane, what are you talking about? What problem?" Eileen demanded.

"Eileen...I don't know how to say this any other way...you were having very serious problems with your sister, okay? I know this, and I know this would not normally be any of my business but—"

"Diane! Where did you hear this? What are you talking about?" insisted Eileen, but as soon as the question was out of her mouth they both looked knowingly at one another. Dr. Thomas sat back in her chair, a sympathetic (or maybe apologetic) expression surfacing as she recognized the breach of faith she was now party to. Eileen looked down and shook her head from side to side in disgust.

"Eileen..." Dr. Thomas began softly, "she wasn't telling me this to get you into any kind of trouble. She insisted that I not share this with you—"

"So you betray her confidence just as she betrayed mine. Is that it? Makes things even, I guess," Eileen said bitterly.

"Eileen, she is a good friend. She was concerned about you. Everyone should have a friend like her. She cares a lot about you. She wanted you to get help and she didn't know what to do. She seemed so upset that—well—I'm the one who pulled this out of her. It's my fault. She was talking about a referral for you to talk to someone and—I don't know—it just seemed, she just seemed really worried about you. I wanted to know what was going on."

Eileen shut her eyes tightly and waved one hand at Dr. Thomas as if to swat away her words. "She had no business sharing personal information about me with anyone. Anyone!" insisted Eileen, her face reddened with anger.

Dr. Thomas leaned forward and said, "When I heard what you were going through, it immediately occurred to me that dealing with that kind of personal problem could—I'm not saying it did—but *could* interfere with your judgment or concentration or whatever.

"Eileen, I just thought that if there were any problems with the way the Pagnotti case was handled in these last few weeks...well... that kind of mishandling..." she hesitated, then continued, "in my opinion...well let's just say I'd be very upset if that's what happened in this case."

"Diane, I can't believe what you're saying!" Eileen shouted.

"Eileen, please understand—"

"Understand? *Understand*? Thanks for your vote of confidence, Diane. I really can't believe this. I can't believe this. What happens in my personal life is none of anyone's business, Diane—"

"Wrong! It's none of anyone's business until it affects *someone else's* life, Eileen. That's my point." Dr. Thomas declared, sitting up straight, glaring at Eileen, whose own face burned with indignation.

"Well why don't you talk to Dr. Levinson after I present the case. I'm sure if there's a problem, he'll let you know," Eileen retorted as she stood up and walked to the door to leave.

As Eileen grasped the doorknob Dr. Thomas called out, "Is it wrong to wonder if you're okay, Eileen? Or if you need some help or some time off? Is that wrong? We're in the mental health field, you know? Are we just supposed to ignore the signs of stress?"

Eileen turned, her eyes burning at Dr. Thomas. She had so many things she wanted to say, but couldn't get it out. She held back, her lips pressed tightly together. She blinked twice very deliberately. Even the thoughts that raced through her mind seemed to stammer and stutter. She wasn't used to expressing anger and didn't know what exactly to say, so she turned and walked out, letting the loud "bang!" of the door speak for her.

The following week, on the day of her Clinical Review Committee meeting, Eileen arrived early. On the previous day, she had spoken to a clinician who'd presented a suicide attempt to the committee six months earlier. Although the clinician described the whole process as "anti-climactic," Eileen remained on edge. She was confident, however, that once she detailed Pagnotti's background and the sessions leading up to his suicide, the committee would have no "quality of care concerns" (a committee euphemism for malpractice). She anxiously looked forward to putting this behind her.

The committee was composed of Dr. Levinson, the medical director, and several supervisors from other programs and departments throughout the mental health center. Dr. Levinson was a husky man in his fifties with a fondness for dark, expensive suits. His yellowish, thinning hair was combed straight back and matched the gold-rimmed glasses he kept perched on the end of his nose. His neatly trimmed mustache and goatee were liberally adorned with gray hairs. Dr. Levinson commanded attention with his steady demeanor and strong speaking style. He spoke directly and bluntly, and although he was soft-spoken, his throaty voice could add import to the most banal conversation.

Eileen glanced at her watch—she was fifteen minutes early—as she entered the third floor conference room where the meeting was to be held. She was not the first to arrive. At the far end of the large, rectangular hardwood table, a young man sat engrossed in a patient's chart, pouring over his notes and scribbling on a pad. Here was someone more anxious than she, Eileen marveled.

Ten minutes later, Dr. Levinson sauntered in carrying several files. Two committee members and his secretary accompanied him.

As they all sat down, the remaining members, who were chatting and laughing in the hallway, finally meandered into the room and took their places around the table. Dr. Levinson introduced the members and gave an overview of the agenda and the process for reporting cases.

He began, "I'd like you to be succinct, okay, but give enough details for us to understand in a logical and orderly way the sequence of events leading up to the incident. You should have received an outline in interoffice mail to guide you along.

"Ms. Duet, did you get an outline?" asked Dr. Levinson.

"Yes, thanks," Eileen replied, holding up the paper.

"And Dr. Weston?" he asked, turning to the young man who continued to read through his patient's chart.

"Yes, I have one, Dr. Levinson," he answered.

"Please try to stick to it, and if the committee has any questions or needs you to fill in any gaps, we'll ask, all right?" explained Dr. Levinson.

"Now, we have a number of length-of-stay cases to review," he continued, "so we need to get started right away. Does either of you have a preference about going first?" he asked, looking back and forth between Eileen and Dr. Weston.

"She can go first," Dr. Weston spoke up, obviously wanting more time to continue obsessing over his notes.

Eileen looked at him then at Dr. Levinson, shrugged her assent and added, "That's fine with me."

Then Eileen lined up Pagnotti's chart next to the one page guideline Dr. Levinson had referred to and began presenting her case. She was anxious, though not in the way she used to feel when she had full-blown panic attacks. Her breathing was erratic as she started reviewing Pagnotti's background, and several times she stopped to swallow fully before resuming. Dr. Levinson listened intently and took notes while Eileen spoke, whereas the other members seemed uninterested, tired, or bored.

Eileen had presented the background and worked her way up to the most recent month, eliciting from the committee no more than a "please speak up" and a few clarifications about Pagnotti's living arrangements. While describing what happened after she had walked Pagnotti over to the emergency room, one of the members, Dr. Hamer, interrupted, "Did you talk to the psychiatrist who released him that day?"

"The one from the emergency room?" asked Eileen.

"Yes," Dr. Hamer answered.

"Well, there was a note in the chart that said Pagnotti was denying any suicidal ideation. He wasn't committable," she explained calmly.

"Yes, he wasn't commitable at that moment because he changed his story as soon as he was in the emergency room. But did you give the psychiatrist the information you had from earlier sessions?" Hamer persisted.

"Well I didn't speak directly to the psychiatrist. I told one of the nurses there; she took down the information, and I assumed she passed it on to the psychiatrist," said Eileen, a defensive edge emerging from her otherwise weak tone. "And when the psychiatrist called me back I let him know that...well...I told him that Pagnotti tends to change his story around...that I thought he was still a risk—"

"Look, she thought he was a risk and she took him over to the ER," Dr. Levinson interjected, trying to move the presentation along and bring some closure. "She went over the clinical with them; that's the way it works. She's not responsible for how they handled it after that."

Eileen nodded in agreement and looked from Dr. Levinson to Hamer, but Hamer's eyes were already averted as if he was no longer interested in the issue he raised.

When Eileen completed her presentation, Dr. Levinson asked the committee if anyone had any remaining questions, or could see any quality of care issues. Most members either didn't respond or simply shook their heads no.

"I think this was a fine and very complete presentation. We appreciate you coming up here to go over this for us," Dr. Levinson stated in his deep, rumbling voice as he looked over the top of his glasses and smiled at Eileen. "I don't hear any quality of care issues. I'll need to look at the chart myself, and then you and I need to set up a separate meeting.

"The only other thing I need you to do is to ask the attending psychiatrist to write the county medical examiner's office requesting a copy of the autopsy report, okay?"

"How does that work?" asked Eileen.

"It's a law in New Jersey. If the attending Psychiatrist simply writes indicating he was Mr. Pagnotti's physician, they'll send a copy of the report. If you need the phone number, just call my secretary. It'll take several weeks, maybe even a couple of months, for the report to be available."

"Okay, that shouldn't be a problem."

"Great. Thank you, Eileen," said Dr. Levinson, and he turned to the rest of the group.

"Thank you," replied Eileen, and she left the conference room exhaling with great relief.

After the presentation to the committee, Eileen's relief quickly turned to anger as she recalled the conversation she had with Dr. Thomas. This in mind, she headed straight to Michelle's office, arriving just as Michelle was ending a session.

"Eileen, how are you?" said Michelle heartily.

"Not good. Can I speak to you for a minute?" asked Eileen, angrily barging into Michelle's office without waiting for a reply.

"Eileen, I have another patient. Can this wait till later?" asked a bewildered Michelle, whose cheery tone had now flattened.

"No, it can't wait," replied Eileen, closing the door and standing nose-to-nose with Michelle.

"I cannot believe you, Michelle. How could you? How could you betray our friendship and talk about something I shared with you in confidence?"

Eileen was incensed, but Michelle remained dumbfounded.

"Eileen, what are you talking about?"

"Michelle, come on! I told you about my sister and you go and tell Diane? I can't believe you would do such a thing! I can't tell you how upset and hurt I am. Did you think that was something for you to just go and...and...and gossip about? You can't stop blabbering for five seconds to protect a friend's privacy?"

"Oh God, Eileen, I am so sorry." Michelle said, staggered by the intensity of Eileen's reaction.

"*Sorry?* Sorry, Michelle? Well sorry doesn't get rid of the humiliation, ya' know."

"Eileen, I had no idea she would...Eileen, I was trying to figure out how to help you—"

"That's how you help? By blabbering all over about my personal life?" Eileen interrupted, her voice growing louder with each exclamation.

"Eileen, listen to me—"

"I'm listening, Michelle. I'm waiting to hear how you can explain this. Do you have any idea how embarrassed I was to have Diane questioning my judgment because...because...because of my sister? I was mortified!"

"Your judgment?" asked Michelle.

"Yes! She took what you told her and turned it into some kind of—I don't know—like I was impaired or something!"

"Impaired?"

"Michelle, she took what you said and somehow figured it might've had something to do with how I handled Pagnotti, like maybe I was so stressed out I couldn't do my job. You know how she is; she was practically blaming me for his suicide!"

"Oh God! Eileen, that's ridiculous!"

"I cannot believe this, Michelle," said Eileen shaking her head. She turned around, walked to the desk and leaned against it momentarily. Almost immediately, she stood up, walked over to the chair and sat down, then stood up and continued pacing like a caged animal.

"Eileen, I am so sorry. I had no idea—this had nothing to do with how you handled the case. Nothing! I was just...you know me, Eileen, I was worrying about you. I was talking to Diane and, well, you know, sort of sharing my concern about you with her—"

"And you had to tell her about my sister?" Eileen shot back. "How the *hell* does worrying about me mean you have to divulge my personal life to her?"

"No, Eileen, it wasn't like that. It's my fault. I know." Then, muttering to herself, "Oh God, I can't believe this."

"Look," Michelle started again, "you know how Diane is. She just...she just seemed to dismiss or minimize what I said when I told her how upset I was about you. But all she knew about was Ron dying awhile back. So she was like...just acting like no big deal, it's a long time ago, and so on.

"I don't know. It was stupid of me, I know," Michelle continued, her body slumping with dejection. "I guess I just felt like she'd be more sympathetic if she knew the bigger picture. God I wish I hadn't, Eileen! I should never have said anything. I am so sorry."

She walked over to Eileen who had stopped pacing and reached out with her hand, but Eileen ignored her sympathetic gesture and walked quickly toward the door.

"Thanks, Michelle," she said sarcastically without turning.

"Eileen..." Michelle pleaded softly, but Eileen had already flung the door shut.

Michelle was crushed by what she'd done, but more than crushed she was shocked that Dr. Thomas had gone right to Elaine and interpreted the information in such a self-serving way. Dr. Thomas cared only about how this incident might affect herself or the clinic, Michelle thought. Instead of hearing the information as Eileen's desperate plea for help, Dr. Thomas heard only the possibility that she—the supervisor—somehow may have let an impaired therapist continue to work.

Michelle had wanted only to help; instead she had added to the web of problems that enveloped her friend's life. She shook her hanging head, chin pressed against her chest, and began to cry.

Chapter Fifteen

DURING THE NEXT WEEK, EILEEN'S ANXIETY LESSENED CONSIDERABLY, and with this relief came an improvement in her treatment of patients. She was attentive to their needs, tuned into their body language and voice tone, confrontational when appropriate, and empathic and supportive when called for. For the first time in what seemed like months, she was able to enjoy her work and feel useful at the end of the day.

She and Michelle had said little to each other since their falling out, which was as pleasing to Eileen as it was agonizing to Michelle. Eileen believed she was standing up for herself for the first time in her life; she felt invigorated, empowered. No longer would she allow others to exploit or abuse her. This of course meant—for the time being at least—that she was cutting off ties with two of the most important people in her life: her sister and her best friend. Because of this, she continued to struggle with bouts of depression. Her thinking had been free of suicide since the meeting with the review committee, but she felt disconnected from everyone and very much alone—a stranger among her colleagues, who gradually reciprocated her coldness as she withdrew into her own world.

Despite her loneliness, dampened mood, and lack of motivation, her days eventually fell into a routine, allowing her to bury the Pagnotti nightmare into the deepest recesses of her mind. Once there, it joined a horde of other distasteful memories that lay dormant (*daddy coming home drunk, daddy's tirade's, daddy hitting mommy, daddy punching holes in the walls*)—out of awareness, but everlasting in their effect.

As the last remnants (the night terrors) came less often, Eileen was beginning to think the whole horrible episode was behind her. Her denial worked wonders until, unfortunately, reality swept back into her life, and the wall she built to imprison this unwanted memory—like so many walls before—turned out to be no more than a house of cards, soon to be scattered on the ground around her.

Friday afternoon around two o'clock, Dr. Thomas, with an unusually formal and curt tone, instructed Eileen to come immediately to her office. When she arrived, Eileen was startled—and instantly dismayed—to see Dr. Levinson, the medical director, as well as Mr. William Strouse, the Vice President of outpatient services together with Dr. Thomas. There they sat stone-faced, while the trembling within Eileen portended the quake to come. She greeted Dr. Levinson by calling him Dr. Levin and nearly tripped over her own feet as she nervously looked for a seat.

Dr. Thomas welcomed her in a muted, though pleasant, tone, but avoided looking directly at her. In fact, all three now seemed to have uncomfortable or queasy expressions on their faces, as if they'd suddenly been struck by food poisoning.

"Is something wrong?" asked Eileen, sitting tentatively on the edge of her seat.

Ignoring her question, Dr. Thomas continued with introductions. "Eileen, you know Dr. Levinson, of course." Eileen and Dr. Levinson smiled and nodded in agreement. "And this is Mr. Strouse the Vice President for outpatient services."

Mr. Strouse, an older man with Owl-like eyes magnified by thick lenses, looked to be in his late sixties or early seventies. He had a full head of white hair and two rather large jowls hanging from his jaw, which gave the impression of a permanent frown. He and Dr. Levinson did nothing but stare at Eileen while Dr. Thomas continued, "Mr. Strouse has met with Mr. Pagnotti, your patient's father."

Eileen's stomach reeled while her pounding heart seemed to clog her throat and left her unable to speak. Her eyes swelled and her breathing halted at the mention of Pagnotti's name. She gaped at her supervisor.

"Mr. Pagnotti made some very serious accusations...and...he... he also brought in some very disturbing—*compelling*—evidence when he met with Mr. Strouse," said Dr. Thomas.

"Evidence?" she breathlessly squeaked at Dr. Thomas, "What evidence? Evidence of what? I don't understand—what did I do? What would he have evidence of?" And without waiting for an answer, she turned and blurted at Mr. Strouse, "Pagnotti's father met with you?"

"That's correct," replied Mr. Strouse in a soft, but starched tone, as he adjusted the heavy glasses on the bridge of his nose.

"What did he want? What's going on?" Eileen asked, frantically shooting glances from Mr. Strouse to Dr. Levinson to Dr. Thomas, each of whom eyed one another. While the others' eyes danced and darted around the room and she waited desperately for a response, Eileen lost all sensation in her legs as her panic heightened.

"Eileen, I feel awful having to ask you this," Dr. Thomas started, struggling to find the right words, "but did...were you...was there any contact between you and Mr. Pagnotti—your patient, not the father—that was...that was..." she paused, looked at Dr. Levinson, then Mr. Strouse and finished, "uh...that did not have something to do with your therapy?"

Terror flooded her veins. Eileen didn't know what they knew or *how* they might know what they know, but her worst fears appeared to be unraveling before her. Her mind raced as she struggled to come up with something to say—something she could *safely* say.

Finally, she offered a stall, "I...I, um, I'm not sure I'm following you. I'm not sure I understand your question." But her pale face, trembling hands, and heavy breathing were obvious to her three interrogators.

"Ms. Duet, look," Dr. Levinson jumped in, "we're not here to crucify you, so please relax. Your presentation the other day was fine. I feel very confident in how this case was—appears to have been—handled. But we do need some clarification—some further information, that's all."

"But I'm not understanding this at all," Eileen persisted with ignorance to their questions. "What information do you need? What did Mr. Pagnotti need? Did he want to speak to me? Is that what he needed?"

"Eileen, Mr. Pagnotti has raised some concerns," said Dr. Thomas sternly. "He believes his son was having a relationship with you. And—"

"A relationship with him! Where did he get that idea?" Eileen shouted.

"Eileen, this is not easy for any of us—"

"What exactly did he say?"

"Let me say this, Eileen. Just let me finish the whole thing. We'll have plenty of time to discuss this," said Dr. Thomas. She paused, looked at the others then at Eileen and continued, "It's Mr. Pagnotti's belief that you had a relationship with his son, and that when you or he...or whoever ended it—"

"*Ended* it? Diane!" Eileen cried out.

"PLEASE! Eileen, let me finish! When it was over—this relationship or whatever it was—well, this is what Mr. Pagnotti believes pushed his son over the edge."

Eileen wriggled and squirmed in her chair while Dr. Thomas spoke. Her hands slapped her lap; her lips squeezed tightly together and at times shot open as she gaped in disbelief at her accusers.

When Dr. Thomas finished, Eileen jumped up from her chair and started yelling, "This is unbelievable! Diane, this is ridiculous! You let my patient's father come in here to blame me for his son's death? His son who was an almost constant suicide risk throughout his treatment here? Was I to blame for his suicidal thoughts the day he walked in here? Was I?" she protested, firmly entrenched in denial at this point. "I can't believe you could entertain this man's delusion!" she continued with her outburst.

"Listen, Eileen," Dr. Thomas declared assertively as she looked grimly at Eileen, "give me more credit than that. Do you think we'd just let some guy waltz in here with some story like that and we believe him? Believe me, Eileen, if anyone wanted this to be some guy's delusion it was me. But you haven't heard everything, and we haven't heard everything, and this isn't something that'll just go away. You're not the only one who has to defend herself." And with her hand waving through the air dramatically, she continued, "This entire Mental Health Center is liable for this kind of malpractice—"

"Malpractice? Malpractice? Are you serious, Diane?"

"Yes, Eileen, malpractice. That's exactly what it is when a therapist gets involved inappropriately with a patient and that patient ends up committing suicide," she shot back.

"Diane! Come on! Inappropriate relationship? Is this for real? I—I...So you're all here basically to tell me you believe what this man told you? I'm guilty first and now have to prove my innocence? Is that what's going on here?" cried Eileen disgustedly, looking across the room at their expressionless faces.

But she knew she was caught. Exactly how, she didn't know, but her stomach churned with fear as she did her best to feign shock and anger.

"Stop it, Eileen. You're not 'guilty.' We're not here to judge you now. But we do have to do the responsible thing. You're going to have to stop seeing patients until this gets clarified," said Dr. Thomas.

"I'm suspended?" Eileen asked, stunned.

"For the time being...I'm afraid so," replied Dr. Thomas.

"I can't believe this," Eileen repeated several times while shaking her head.

No one said a word. They sneaked quick peeks at Eileen, but mostly looked to the side or at the floor. Eileen's pleading look at Dr. Thomas nearly grabbed hold of her, but Dr. Thomas, too, kept her gaze averted.

The silence congealed the tension in the room to the point of suffocation, at which point Eileen jumped up and walked to the door. Before leaving, she turned around and asked, "Do I need to get a lawyer?"

"You don't need a lawyer, Ms. Duet," said Dr. Levinson, shaking his head and offering a strained smile. "The Center has legal services that we'll consult. Mr. Pagnotti has retained a lawyer, so this could get fairly complicated."

"A lawyer? He went to a lawyer?" asked Eileen.

Dr. Levinson nodded yes and continued, "We're going to need your cooperation, though. These next couple of weeks are going to be quite busy, and legal services will probably—not probably, definitely—want to talk to you at some point."

"Ms. Duet," added Mr. Strouse, "we want you to understand that we're here to support you. As Dr. Thomas said, we're not here to judge you. We're just going to need as much information about what happened in order for us to...well, in order to get this Pagnotti guy to realize it's not worth it for him to pursue this. And we'd like to keep this from getting any publicity or getting to the newspapers."

"The newspapers!" Eileen cried out, and then looking at Dr. Thomas, she asked, "This isn't going to be in the newspapers, is it, Diane?"

"Well I would hope not," answered Dr. Thomas. "But I can't account for what Mr. Pagnotti will do."

"Look, forget about the newspapers, okay?" Dr. Levinson jumped in sounding annoyed. "Let's just focus on getting our act together and consulting with our lawyer, and clarifying the facts of the case."

Then turning to Eileen, Dr. Levinson said, "Ms. Duet, why don't you go home and get some rest. We're going to meet with you toward the end of next week. There's no sense worrying about this now. There isn't anything anyone can do right now, okay?"

"That's easy for you to say," Eileen remarked with sarcasm.

"I'm sorry. I don't mean you're not going to worry about this, Ms. Duet; I know this is upsetting. But there's nothing we can do right now."

"Eileen, I just needed to inform you about the investigation and about your suspension," Dr. Thomas said. "We can't get into any details until we've met with the lawyers. So let's end this now and we'll be in touch with you next week, okay?"

"So I should leave immediately, Diane?" Eileen asked, her voice tinged with bitterness.

"Eileen, you don't have to run out of here *immediately*. But the suspension goes into effect first thing Monday morning," Dr. Thomas answered, feigning a sympathetic smile.

Eileen turned and walked out the door. She heard Dr. Thomas pull the door shut and imagined how they were now going to discuss her, as well as whatever else Pagnotti's father had said to Mr. Strouse. She was shaking. She had no idea how or what Mr. Pagnotti knew regarding what happened between her and his son, but she was overwhelmed with a fear of the worst. They knew something. But how, she asked herself over and over again. She began to cry, standing in the hallway—shaking and crying.

Eileen gathered her belongings, finished writing several progress notes and eventually left the building a little after five o'clock. She drove home with a great burden lifted from her.

Having decided to stop this situation from destroying her piece by piece, she once again convinced herself that ending her own life was the answer—the final solution to her problems. There was no going back on this now; and with this commitment came a sense of tranquillity—an internal silence and a sense of finality. She would not have to face the committee again, or answer their questions, and she would escape the ultimate humiliation. It was over.

When she arrived home, Eileen was astonished to find her mother—*of all people*—standing by her parked car in the driveway. She hadn't seen her mother since just after Ron's death and their conversation about Kelly.

"Mom, what's the matter? What are you doing here?" Eileen asked.

"Is that how you greet me, 'what's the matter?' How about 'I'm so glad to see you'" she said, and it was possible she was teasing, though it was always so hard to decipher her tone.

Eileen was confused, and her expression wasn't lost on her mother, who waved her hand—"Oh, forget that"—and then suddenly hugged her daughter and asked, "Can we go inside? I'm cold."

"How long have you been here?" Eileen asked as they walked inside.

"Not long. I figured I'd meet you just after work. Why are you wearing this light jacket? Don't you know they're calling for snow?"

"Oh mom," sighed Eileen with a sweeping roll of her eyes. "I'm not your little girl anymore, you know."

"You never stop being a mother's little girl, Eileen," her mother replied as they walked to the kitchen.

As Eileen filled the kettle with water and placed it on the stove to boil, her mother sat down and continued, "You never stop being a little girl, Eileen, but sometimes moms stop acting like moms. Or I should say, in some cases moms never *start* being moms."

She chuckled and shrugged her shoulders as Eileen whirled around and looked at her with eyebrows raised up high in wonder at her mother's contrite tone.

"What's going on, mom?" asked Eileen as she sat down next to her mother.

"I know, I know, this must sound odd to hear me talk this way-"

"No—well yeah—but not odd in a bad way; this is good...I...I'm just....Well, did something happen? Is everything okay?"

"Last week I went to a funeral," her mother began.

"Oh, I'm sorry. Who died?" asked Eileen.

"Remember my friend, Holly?"

"Holly? Mrs. Davenport?"

"Yes, Mrs. Davenport—"

"Oh god, the one who used to live behind you, who was always sick?"

"No, no, it's not Holly who died. Holly who's so sick is still alive and kicking, God bless her. Holly had a daughter Kate, and Kate and Holly had the most incredible relationship. They weren't like mother and daughter, you know; they were more like sisters—best friends, her mother said, her eyes wide, unblinking, and glassy. She looked away momentarily and rubbed a tear away with one finger.

Eileen reached out sympathetically to hold her mother's hand, but the whistling tea kettle interrupted her. She jumped up to turn off the flame, but left the kettle on the stove so she could sit back down with her mother.

"Kate died, Eileen," her mother said her eyes now welling up with tears. "Some...I don't know, kidney problem or something."

"Oh mom, I'm so sorry," Eileen said leaning forward to hug her. "I didn't realize you were so close. This is really upsetting you, isn't it?"

"I haven't stopped thinking about it. It's been on my mind constantly."

"Mom, I'm so sorry for you. How is Mrs. Davenport doing?" asked Eileen.

"She's hanging in there. But Eileen, that's not what I wanted to talk about. That's not what's got my mind so...so...so flustered. It's not that they we were *that* close; that's not it."

"What then? What is it?"

"You know, here's Mrs. Davenport with this great relationship... this unbelievable relationship right there with her all the time—of course I'm sure they had their little squabbles too, just as every family does—but...what does she have now? What? Gone, just like that," her mother said, snapping her fingers. "And here I am with..." she paused. "...with a daughter who...well let's face it, we have *no* relationship. I have two living daughters, but I'm...I'm really dead to both of you."

She paused as she searched to find the right words. Eileen started to speak, but her mother held up a hand to hush her and continued, "And I know, I know, Eileen, that I am a big part of that, a big part of the reason why our relationship is so lousy."

"Mom—" Eileen began but was cut off again.

"No, Eileen, let me finish. I've been thinking about this a long time now and I need to say this to you," her mother insisted, speaking with an unsteady voice yet a commanding tone. "I lived my whole life concerned more about what things *should* be like, and how people *should* be, and how a daughter of mine *should* act, that I never bothered to get to know—to *really know*—either of you. I cannot believe, when I look back on my life, that I let your father do the things he did to me. I can't believe that that was me. I mean...maybe I'm not explaining this right or maybe it doesn't make sense, but it's like I can look back at what I did and yet, the person I recall doing those things—that wasn't me. Or at least, I don't want to think it was me.

She paused for a moment and looked intently at Eileen, who was dumbfounded by her mother's revelations. Eileen was not about to interrupt. She caressed her mother's hand as they continued to look into each other's eyes.

"Oh listen to me now; I'm sounding like the therapist with all this *analysis* of myself."

They both smiled, and she continued. "The real me, Eileen, wants to get to know her daughter—not the daughter I thought you ought to be or should have been or that I expected you to be. No...I want to get to know you.

"I can't undo the mistakes I've made. But I can stop trying to make you into some stupid fantasy, some ideal that I carried around in my head. I can get to know the you that's right here with me— the you I can touch, the you I can listen to and learn from."

"Oh my God, Mom. I—I think I'm speechless," Eileen said as she laughed through her tears and hugged her mother.

"I love you, Eileen. I really do. I've always loved you. I just...I don't know—"

"You don't have to say anything else, Mom," Eileen jumped in, again hugging her mother tightly. "I love you too, Mom. I want to make this work too."

They hugged some more and cried and laughed and talked. They talked until almost midnight. Eileen divulged to her mother that she had been suspended indefinitely while the investigation of her patient's suicide proceeded. Although she confided in her about the suicide, the investigation, and her suspension, she was reluctant to discuss any of the allegations of the inquiry—about the chatting with Pagnotti and about stupidly agreeing to meet him outside Macy's.

Her mother agreed to stay the night, and the next morning they made plans for Eileen to stay at her mother's place for a few days. This sudden turn of events may very well have saved Eileen's life as her suicide plan was placed on hold for the time being.

On Wednesday, Eileen checked her messages and discovered that Dr. Thomas had called late Tuesday night. When she returned the call, she was informed of a mandatory meeting on Thursday regarding the "incident," as Dr. Thomas called it. The anxiety returned and she felt trapped, despite having previously decided she would not have to face the committee ever again.

Despite a resolution to end her life (*Not just yet. I still have time to get it done*), the next morning she kissed her mother and thanked her for the most "important three days of my life." She gathered her belongings and stopped at home before heading to the meeting. Her curiosity about the meeting and what they might have to say had successfully won over her suicidal impulses—for the time being at least.

Although she was nervous, she really had no idea what the Review Committee had in store for her. She knew Mr. Pagnotti had provided some kind of information and had made some accusations, but she couldn't imagine what or how much the committee actually knew. Maybe they needed for her only to reassure them that the case was handled appropriately. Maybe, she thought, she would be back at work the very next week. Maybe not.

Chapter Sixteen

ILEEN ARRIVED AT WORK AND MADE HER WAY THROUGH THE HALLS toward the conference room. Her eyes staring straight ahead as she walked, she felt as if she were on stage: voices hushed, heads turned toward her, and others seemed to motion in her direction. Or maybe it was just her imagination.

She didn't know why, but she took a small detour to stop at her office first. It looked the same as it did a week ago, just after the meeting with Drs. Levinson and Thomas and Mr. Strouse—the meeting when she learned of her suspension. She sat for a moment to get her breath. Fragments of thoughts began percolated and evaporated. Images flashed before her—as she focused on one issue, another came to mind. Efforts to keep her mind focused on just one idea at a time were futile.

She hadn't yet prepared herself for this meeting—how to respond to their questions, what to admit to, how to explain herself. This was partly because she had no idea *what* they would ask or what information they already had.

Her head ached, and as she reached in the drawer for a couple of Advil, the phone rang, startling her. She answered it with a breathless "hello" and was pleased to hear Mary's familiar voice.

"Hey Eileen, Dr. Thomas thought you might be in your office. She said they're waiting for you. You were supposed to be here like fifteen minutes ago."

"Fifteen minutes ago? Are you sure? I thought I was like fifteen minutes early. God, thanks so much, Mary. I'll get right over there. Thank you."

"Oh, and Eileen?"

"Yes?"

"It's good to hear your voice again," Mary said with a friendly chuckle.

"Mary...thank you so much. That is really sweet of you. It's nice hearing you as well."

Eileen hung up, wiped a tear from her eye, and rushed over to the conference room.

Dr. Levinson, Dr. Thomas, and Mr. Strouse were seated around the table, along with one unfamiliar face, which Eileen seemed to stare at as she entered the room.

"Eileen, this is Ms. Giordani," Dr. Thomas said immediately, standing and pointing her hand in the direction of a smartly dressed, attractive, dark-haired woman who appeared to be in her forties. Ms. Giordani wore a dark gray suit and had a broad smile with lot's of teeth that she displayed proudly as she offered her hand to Eileen.

"Please, it's Annette. Nice to meet you," Ms. Giordani said in a cutesy, sing-song voice that was so incongruous with her appearance that it seemed dubbed over her natural voice.

"It's nice to meet you, too," Eileen said softly, accepting Ms. Giordani's handshake.

"Eileen, Annette is from the Center's legal services," Dr. Thomas began. "She's reviewed some of the material for us and has spoken to a number of people—"

"A number of people? What people?" asked Eileen defensively.

"Mr. Pagnotti is suing the Center for his son's suicide; actually, for malpractice," answered Dr. Thomas. "His lawyers will be talking to a *lot* of people and going through all the same papers we'll have access to, including the entire chart. Annette has begun a preliminary investigation to give us some idea of what we may face."

Looking down at the table with a heavy sigh before looking sternly at Eileen, Dr. Thomas continued, "Eileen, I am very, very concerned about what went on here. Outraged is a word that comes to—"

Dr. Thomas, Dr. Levinson interrupted, holding his thick hand up to halt her. I think it's best we do what we have to do first—"

"I apologize, Dr. Levinson," Dr. Thomas reacted quickly. Then turning again to Eileen and speaking in a softer tone, continued, "Disappointed, okay? I'm just disappointed, Eileen."

Eileen, wide-eyed, looked at Dr. Thomas then scanned the other faces in the room before looking somewhere in the middle of the table in front of her, her eyes glazed over, and her neck stiffened. She pulled her thighs tightly together to stop their shaking.

"Eileen, I need you to be frank and forthright. This is not the time to hide anything, okay?" Ms. Giordani said in her squeaky voice.

"Hide? What would I hide, Ms. Giordani," Eileen snapped.

"Oh, well...I...well, I certainly wouldn't expect you to *hide* anything," Ms. Giordani reassured her with a toothy smile. "I just want you to understand that *we* are not the adversary right now. We're in this together, and the best way for us to defend ourselves is...well...I need to ask you some questions."

"That's fine," Eileen replied more calmly, her eyes shooting around the room to judge the others' reactions and expressions.

There was a pause while Ms. Giordani shuffled through her papers. After several tense moments of what seemed like directionless fiddling, she started rather abruptly, knocking the breath out of Eileen as if she'd landed a blow at her midsection: "Eileen, did you have email correspondence with your patient, Mr. Pagnotti?"

"Email correspondence?" Eileen choked, but her feigned puzzlement wasn't going over well with Dr. Thomas who shifted noisily in her seat.

"Ms. Duet," Ms. Giordani said with a patronizing smile and tone, "do you need me to explain again why we're here?"

"I understand why we're here, Ms. Giordani. I wasn't exactly sure what you meant by 'email correspondence.' If I understand you correctly ...then, no, I did not correspond with Mr. Pagnotti by email," Eileen responded sharply.

"Well evidently you weren't answering your email, Ms. Duet. Mr. Pagnotti's father has shown us at least one copy of an email that links your name, Eileen Duet, to a screen name or some kind of nickname that you went by. I—believe—" She paused as she leafed through more papers. "Yes, here it is: *Cheeryl*," Ms. Giordani said, her voice rising even higher with annoyance.

"Ms. Giordani—" Eileen began, her face reddening. Then turning to Dr. Thomas, she continued, "Diane, I never once responded to *any* email that he sent me, not one."

"Oh Eileen!" Dr. Thomas exclaimed, "What was he doing with your email address to begin—"

"Wait, wait, wait, hold on, please," Ms. Giordani interjected, looking at Dr. Thomas. "Please let me finish." And she turned back to Eileen: "Ms. Duet, you *were* corresponding with Mr. Pagnotti over a chat line, were you not?"

"A chat line?" Dr. Thomas spoke up before a stunned Eileen could close her gaping mouth to reply.

"On the computer, you know, typing in messages back and forth to one another," Ms. Giordani explained to Dr. Thomas. And then to Eileen, "You may not have been corresponding through email—if it's true, as you say, that you didn't reply to his messages—but Mr. Pagnotti has several pages of text that he pulled off his son's computer. You did reply or chat back and forth, did you not, Ms. Duet? I believe the nickname he used was Sweetdude or Sweetdude35?"

Eileen's mouth closed and she swallowed hard, but said nothing. Her shoulders moved up and down rhythmically as her breathing became deeper and more rapid. She looked directly at Ms. Giordani, whose steely eyes locked onto hers. She couldn't bear to turn her crimson face, burning with humiliation, in Dr. Thomas's direction. The room felt as if it were spinning.

"You *were* chatting online regularly with your patient, were you not, Ms. Duet?" Ms. Giordani repeated more softly now, which took a little of the squeak out of her tone. "I mean, unless you're going to tell me you weren't "Cheeryl," but of course that could easily be traced. And besides, there's more than a dozen email messages he sent with your name on them—and he alternates between calling you by your name and by the nickname, "Cheeryl." So I think it's best if you explain what this was about so we can figure out how—"

"I didn't know it was him! I didn't know it was my patient! I swear, Ms. Giordani!" Eileen erupted, crying out as she hid her face in her hands.

"Ms. Duet," Dr. Levinson began in his gruff, yet steadying voice, "are you saying you had no idea you were chatting with Mr. Pagnotti, your patient? That—"

"I'm afraid that's impossible," Ms. Giordani scoffed, then she sarcastically asked, "did you not know it was your patient you were chatting with after you met him outside Macy's, Ms. Duet?"

Eileen lifted her pale, tear-stained face from her hands and looked around at their faces, which were as astounded as hers, while Ms. Giordani now nimbly pulled out and passed a copy of text to Dr. Levinson, who handed it to Mr. Strouse, who in turn handed it to Dr. Thomas:

> *...Sweetdude35>* Well we don't have to go into the mall. I thought we were just using that as a landmark. We can meet right in front of Macy's and then we'll find a diner or someplace to go get

coffee. Since the mall is closed we won't have any problem finding each other right in front.

Cheeryl> Hmmmmm...

Sweetdude35> Hmmmmm? Come on, no hmmmmm, let's just do it, otherwise we'll chicken out if we wait. Let's just go on our instincts.

Sweetdude35> Can you hold on one second. I'm being interrupted.

Sweetdude35> Listen, let's just do it. Let's meet now. I can be there in half an hour. How about you?

Cheeryl> Let's go! I'll meet you right in front of Macy's in thirty minutes.

Sweetdude35> Let's do it. Thirty minutes to Macy's! Meet you then, Cheeryl...

"This is *un-be*-liveable!" Dr. Thomas cried out, raising her voice with each syllable, her lips wrinkled in disgust as if she'd bitten a lemon. "Eileen, this is just outrageous. OUTRAGEOUS! I am really disappointed," she said shaking her head as she passed the paper along to Eileen.

Eileen looked at it briefly, horrified to see her words—their free-flowing back and forth—captured like a snapshot on a piece of paper. What had been a two-way conversation with line after line of comments continuously being added in a dynamic—and at times emotional—give and take was now reduced to dry text, laid out in its entirety—stripped of emotion and attitude and tone. She was mortified and sickened by what she read. Without finishing, she pushed the paper away and looked around the table at three staring faces.

"Ms. Giordani, this is not...I need to explain," Eileen said, fighting back tears, her stomach wrenched in a knot. "This is not what it looks like," she pleaded, even though her own ears told her she sounded as pathetic and disgraceful as an unfaithful spouse caught in bed with her lover.

"Oh please, Eileen! We're not fools!" Dr. Thomas shouted. "What do you take us for—a bunch of idiots?"

Eileen's eyes shot open wide in fear and her body shivered uncontrollably to Dr. Thomas's bellowing voice. She had never before seen Dr. Thomas so enraged.

"You were having these...these, these *chat* sessions, and you're going to tell us you didn't know it was your patient you were writing to? Is that it? Are you kidding?"

"Dr. Thomas—" Dr. Levinson tried unsuccessfully to interrupt.

"And what are you going to tell us now, Eileen, that you didn't mean to arrange a get-together with him? Do you have any idea, ANY IDEA how this looks? Eileen, you arranged to meet your patient for a date—A DATE! You were chatting back and forth, over *who knows* how long, while you were seeing him in therapy! What were you thinking? Where was your head?" she yelled, bouncing her index finger off her forehead. "I can't believe this. I really can't believe this."

"Please, Dr. Thomas, Please!" Dr. Levinson again tried unsuccessfully to calm her.

"I'm sorry, Dr. Levinson, but do you have any idea the position this puts the mental health center in?" Dr. Thomas growled, her face red and the vein along the side of her neck bulging as she carried on.

"I understand, Dr. Thomas, but—" Dr. Levinson again tried to interject.

"It's bad enough she's carrying on a relationship with one of her patients, but this suicide puts us in a completely indefensible position. This is disgraceful! This is malpractice, Eileen. They're going to say he committed suicide because you broke off the relationship. They'll say you took advantage of an emotionally unstable person. This is a disgrace."

And with the last words spewed out, Dr. Thomas stood and walked away from the table to pour a cup of coffee at the back of the room.

Eileen looked at the others, then managed to say to Ms. Giordani, "I *did not* break up with Mr. Pagnotti, Ms. Giordani. We were not having...we *never* had any kind of a relationship. I need to explain this."

Ms. Giordani feigned a sympathetic smile as the room remained silent, waiting to hear Eileen's explanation.

"I...when I met Mr. Pagnotti outside Macy's I had no idea that he was the person I was meeting," Eileen began.

"You're saying that the entire time you were chatting, you had no idea it was your patient, Ms. Duet?" Mr. Strouse said, speaking for the first time and with a somewhat reassuring yet cautious tone.

"That's right. And as soon as I realized who I was meeting, I left and never chatted again with him and never met him again," Eileen replied.

"Except that you continued in therapy with him and never mentioned any of this to me or to any administrator," Dr. Thomas called out from the other end of the room.

"Ms. Giordani?" Dr. Levinson said, ignoring Dr. Thomas and soliciting a reply from the lawyer.

"Well, Ms. Duet, are you saying that after you met Mr. Pagnotti outside Macy's you never met him again—in an out-of-work setting, that is?" Ms. Giordani asked.

"Ms. Giordani, that was the only time we met, and that was by mistake. We never met again. Never. I swear! I was *not* having a relationship with my patient. That's the point I'm trying to make. I chatted with someone I knew only as Sweetdude35. I had no idea—"

"One second, Ms. Duet. Hold on. There was one other time."

"One other time? No there wasn't," Eileen insisted with a puzzled look.

"See, this is the thing, Ms. Duet. We need your cooperation and your honesty—"

"Ms. Giordani, I really resent your questioning my honesty here."

"Ms. Duet, Mr. Pagnotti's lawyers will have no problem gathering information about visitors to your home."

"Visitors to my home?" Eileen squealed in disbelief.

"That's right, Ms. Duet, visitors to your home. When I first sent out an investigator, I planned for him to speak to several of your neighbors—"

"You spoke to my neighbors!" Eileen exclaimed.

"Eileen, as I was saying, we planned to speak to several, but stopped immediately after the first one. We were simply trying to find out if anyone had ever seen Mr. Pagnotti's son's old, beat up, gray Nissan Sentra around here. And guess what? He *was* at your house, wasn't he, Eileen. And the one occasion we know about, happened not too long before his suicide. And it happened *after* the meeting at Macy's," Ms. Giordani finished with a dramatic slap of the table.

Eileen began to cry. She felt overwhelmed, and she felt trapped. She felt trapped by the circumstances and facts, which on the surface were objectively true. But she was too unnerved and too distraught to fully explain how things turned out the way they did. And worse than that, she felt attacked and unsupported by the very people who said that they were "in this together," and who supposedly wanted to "defend OURselves."

"Ms. Giordani," Eileen began, struggling for her breath between tears, "he was terrorizing me! He wasn't visiting me. He just came to my house on his own...I thought he was going to kill me! Or rape me! I didn't invite him. You MUST believe me!"

"He broke into your house and threatened you?" Dr. Levinson asked.

"Yes, yes!" Eileen replied.

"Did you call the police, Ms. Duet?" Ms. Giordani asked skeptically.

"No, I couldn't. I couldn't because I was afraid. Don't you understand?" Eileen replied angrily through tears.

"Afraid?" Dr. Levinson asked. "After he left your house, you were afraid to call the police or tell anyone?"

"I was afraid no one would believe me, just like right now. This is exactly what I was afraid of."

"We wouldn't believe you, Eileen?" Dr. Thomas said incredulously as she finally returned to her seat at the conference table. "Your patient breaks into your house and we wouldn't believe you? But you have this ongoing *chat* thing happening, and you arrange to meet with him and you expect us to believe that you didn't know who you were arranging to meet? You must be kidding!

"I can't believe that you *wouldn't* report your patient showing up at your house and 'terrorizing' you, as you say, unless there was something already going on—something that you didn't want any of us to find out about. I'm sorry, Eileen, but this is just too unbelievable. You better come up with something better than that," Dr. Thomas scoffed.

"But that's exactly my point," Eileen declared. "There *was* something going on. I had been chatting with this stranger and it turned out to be him, but I didn't know it was him until after I saw him...after we met. I swear it! I was humiliated. I was so embarrassed. Diane, you have to believe me. I didn't want *any* of this coming out. I wanted it all to go away."

"I must admit, the more I hear, the more preposterous it all sounds," Mr. Strouse commented. "This just doesn't look good."

"Frankly, I don't get it all, myself," Dr. Levinson added, "but there's a lot of information here, and I think we all need to sit on this for a little bit."

"Ms. Duet, I am inclined to believe what you say," Ms. Giordani said, eliciting surprised looks from everyone in the room. "But I'm playing devil's advocate here because you have to understand how this looks."

"I know, I know," Eileen said, sounding defeated.

"Page after page of chatting that he saved, and then the two of you meeting, and his car being ID'ed outside your house; and then not too long after his car being at your house he commits suicide," Ms. Giordani said. "It looks real bad."

"Why don't we bring this to an end. Eileen, we'll need you to be available if we have to reach you," Dr. Levinson said.

"And Eileen, please keep this to yourself for now. I am not about to share any of this with the staff, and I trust that you won't either. We don't need rumors flying around here," Dr. Thomas explained.

Eileen stood up wearily and dragged herself out the door. She headed down the hallway, downstairs and past the cafeteria when Michelle intercepted her just as she was on her way out the door. Eileen was curt with her, offered no information about the meeting, and declined Michelle's offer to call her or to stop by later. "You've already done your share of help, Michelle," she said derisively as she walked out the door. She got into her car and drove off.

Chapter Seventeen

C OLD FINGERS ON ONE HAND GRIPPED THE STEERING WHEEL WHILE her other hand fumbled stiffly to start the engine. A mix of sleet and snow were falling from the dark gray sky as Eileen's car slipped and skidded out of the parking lot and onto the main road. She hunched forward and squinted at the road ahead of her while the wipers scraped rhythmically across the crust of ice that had formed on the windshield.

There was no way to explain her way out of this, she thought despondently. *All that email he saved! And the chatting!* No one would ever believe her. *How could they? He came to my house; they know he was there, and I didn't tell ANYONE! How could I have been so stupid? Why did I agree to meet him? How stupid! How stupid, stupid stupid!*

She felt that trapped, panicky feeling creeping quickly up on her, beginning to smother her again, her mind swarming with self-loathing thoughts and guilt; but the more she thought about her situation, the more clearly she saw a way out—*the* way out. She wouldn't have to answer to anyone. She wouldn't have to face the committee and listen to Dr. Thomas's scolding or Ms. Giordani's irritating voice and her dogged attempts to expose and embarrass her: The worst had come true and now she would wipe the slate clean. When she thought about suicide, the panic began to subside; there was a sense of closure, of finality.

Her car slid to a stop at an intersection. She looked around at the empty roads and after a brief pause, drove through the red light. Her fingertips were numb as she gripped so tightly to the wheel that her knuckles felt as though they were going to pop when she finally arrived home and screeched to a halt in her driveway.

She carefully trod across the icy walkway to the front door and let herself in. Without taking off her coat, she headed straight for the medicine cabinet in the downstairs bathroom. She found a large half-filled bottle of Advil, grabbed it and made her way to the refrigerator, where she pulled out a nearly full bottle of white wine. She sat down at the kitchen table and struggled with her thawing fingers to remove the cap from the Advil.

The cap finally popped loose, and she dumped the contents onto the table. She looked at the pile of little white pills and then spread them out so each one lay flat on the table. She counted twenty five of them. Then she pulled the cork from the wine bottle, got up from the table to get a glass, and sat back down to fill it with wine. She filled a water glass about half-full, brought it to her lips and started sipping. As the wine passed across her tongue, she opened her mouth more widely and began to gulp it down, stopping momentarily as she choked from drinking too fast.

She set the glass down and looked at the pills. She wondered if she should take a handful or just two at a time. Realizing how nonsensical her decision was in light of what she was doing, she impulsively grabbed about three pills and washed them down with another mouthful of wine. She quickly guzzled what remained in her glass, then poured another. She took five more pills, washed them down with a gulp of wine and took five more.

As she continued drinking, the image of Brock Pagnotti popped into her head—his sick smile, his dirty face, and his expensive, but poorly tailored suits. She thought of the irony of this whole situation. He couldn't have her while he was alive, so he's dragging her with him into death, she thought. And she chuckled.

She thought about how kind he had been when she thought he was merely a like-minded stranger, lonely and seeking companionship. How amazing, she thought, that he could be so different from the Brock Pagnotti she knew—so understanding, so empathic, and so helpful when she was going through some very rough periods with her husband. Obviously he learned something from therapy, she thought, and then she laughed again. *He couldn't help himself, but he sure as hell helped me for awhile. How ironic. How fucking ironic!*

She was feeling dizzy now, but continued drinking.

Which was the *real* Brock Pagnotti, she wondered—the guy online, Sweetdude35, or the enraged, suicidal pain-in-the-ass that she saw in therapy? Ah, what a tangled web the Internet turned out to be...so vast, so complex, so many millions of people across the world...and she ends up connecting with her patient! *Of all people... HIM!* She laughed out loud now, and then reached for two more pills and a swig of the wine.

He wasn't who he said he was, and I wasn't who I said I was either, she thought. Come to think of it, there are a lot of people who aren't who they say they are. And not all of them are anonymous chatters on the Internet. She thought about her sister and her husband and about the double lives they lived, and about the phony front her mother hid behind during all those years she was being abused. And she thought about the smiling facade she was forced to wear throughout her childhood—a facade she used so no one would know about her alcoholic father and, more importantly, so he wouldn't turn his abuse on her. And there was Michelle, whom she thought was her friend, her confidante, sharing personal information about her with Dr. Thomas.

The whole world can go to hell, she thought. *They're all a bunch of phonies!* As she lifted her glass of wine to finish it off, she caught a glimpse in the corner of her eye of the red blinking light from the answering machine. She stopped at once and stumbled from the table to play the message. It was her mother calling to see how she was doing.

Panic set in as this incidental event—a small and fleeting piece of reality—seemed to jar her momentarily from the dreamlike state she had drifted into. It was strange, but somehow her mother's voice on the machine caused her to see herself from an outsider's vantagepoint. She saw herself in the act of committing suicide and thought at once of what her mother would think. Staring at the blurry phone, her head still swimming with confusion, she decided (realized?) she didn't want to die...not just yet. *How stupid this is! What was I thinking? What am I doing to myself!* "I don't want to die! I DON'T WANT TO DIE!" she cried out to the empty house.

Frantic, she dialed her mother's house. "Please, please, mom, come over right away!"

"Eileen, what's the matter? Are you okay?" her mother asked quickly, sensing desperation in her daughter's voice.

"I've done something stupid! Please! I started taking pills, mom. I was drinking wine and taking pills!"

"Eileen! What? Pills? What kind of pills? Oh my God! Eileen, why?"

"Please, it doesn't matter! Just come over right away! I need you to drive me to the emergency room!"

"Yes...of course, Eileen, of course."

"Mom, I don't wanna die! I DON'T WANNA DIE!" she cried.

"Oh my God, Eileen, I'll be there right away!"

They hung up the phone and Eileen ran to the bathroom where she jabbed her finger down her throat. She wretched and then began vomiting.

Her mother arrived about twenty-five minutes later. She let herself in and rushed into the living room where she found Eileen lying on the couch with her coat still on. She hurried to her side and began shaking her upper arms and tapping her cheek.

"Eileen! Eileen! Honey wake up! Please, wake up!" she yelled.

Eileen seemed groggy and a bit confused when she opened her eyes. Her mother helped her sit up and after a few moments, she stood on her own.

"Honey, are you okay? Can you hear me?"

"Mom..."

"Eileen, can you walk? Are you able to walk?" her mother yelled.

"Yes. Just—let's—just—get—to the car."

They walked out to the car, Eileen stumbling and nearly falling backwards before they got in and drove off.

"How many pills did you take, Eileen? What were you trying to do?" her mother asked, as she sped away from the house.

"I...I'm not sure...maybe...well, I took just a couple of handfuls I think."

"A couple of handfuls?" her mother exclaimed.

"Not handfuls...like...I took like three or four at a time, but only a few of those. I...I...." She started to nod off.

"Eileen! Eileen, don't fall asleep. Wake up! Wake up!"

She reached over and pushed her gently. Eileen lifted her head up slightly.

"What kind of pills were these, Eileen? What were you taking? Were you taking drugs?"

"No Mom, it wasn't 'drugs.' It was just Advil, but I started drinking a lot of wine with it...Oh mom, I just wanted to die! You have no idea what I've been through," she cried. "I feel sick. I think—I'm—going—to get sick again."

Her mother pulled the car over and stopped. Eileen seemed to need every ounce of strength to open the door so she could lean out and vomit. When she finished, her mother jumped out of the car and ran around to her daughter's side so she could close the door for her. Eileen slouched back in her seat while her mother returned to the driver's side and they continued on their way.

They pulled into the parking lot of the hospital and sat in the car for awhile. Having vomited again, Eileen seemed to have more life, more strength. They began talking. She confessed to her mother all the details of what had happened with her patient: the chatting, meeting outside Macy's, Pagnotti showing up at the house, the suicide and the review committee and her suspension. Her mother listened in utter disbelief.

Eileen was reluctant—now nearly an hour since she downed the pills and wine—to go into the emergency room. She was feeling slightly lightheaded and sleepy, but her stomach didn't bother her at all. Her fear that it was too late and she would die had passed. She was too embarrassed to go into the emergency room and explain that she had tried to overdose on Advil and wine.

Insisting that she wanted her daughter to get checked out, her mother helped concoct a story to tell the doctor. They agreed to tell the doctors she had taken some aspirin after having had some wine, and that it had upset her stomach; therefore, she was worried about the mixing of alcohol and aspirin, and just wanted to make sure she was all right.

They waited two and half hours in the waiting room, nearly half of which Eileen spent sleeping. The doctor asked her several questions, hardly seemed interested in her, and never asked if she had tried to hurt herself or if this was a suicide attempt. It was typical ER treatment, she thought cynically. She wasn't bleeding or dying, so they let her go after a perfunctory review of her presenting complaint and of her vital signs, all of which were normal.

After the visit to the emergency room, Eileen's mother stayed with her for ten days. They spent almost all their time together, reminiscing, crying, laughing, and talking about the future. Time seemed to stand still as the days passed. But on the eleventh day, Dr. Thomas called asking Eileen to come into work that afternoon. Like a flashback, all the old feelings returned in full force. Her stomach tightened, her heart raced. The fact that Dr. Thomas said she had good news didn't seem to lessen the anxiety, but her mother urged her to "do the right thing and see what they have to say."

When Eileen arrived at the mental health center, Dr. Thomas appeared different to her. Her distant, icy manner had been replaced by a more affable, almost jovial welcoming as they walked together into Dr. Thomas's office to sit and talk.

"You look good, Eileen, really."

"Thank you."

"I have some interesting news for you, Eileen," Dr. Thomas began. Eileen stared straight ahead, looking at Dr. Thomas but remaining silent.

"You know that in any completed suicide we always request the autopsy report to confirm the cause of death, right?" Dr. Thomas asked. .

"Yes...that's right...and?" asked Eileen.

"Well, Pagnotti's report came in. I should say, we didn't get the actual report, yet, but the police contacted us. And guess what," Dr. Thomas said with a broad smile. "Your patient didn't commit suicide, Eileen."

"I don't understand," Eileen responded, sitting forward on her seat and squinting at Dr. Thomas.

"This is really quite amazing. Your patient apparently suffered a severe blow to the head, Eileen, which literally cracked the back, lower side of his skull."

"I don't understand," Eileen interrupted. "Did he fall or something? Are they thinking this was an accident?"

"Hold on a sec, this is really unbelievable, seriously. Let me explain. The medical examiner concludes that the bullet passed through from the back to the front of his head, not from the front or side, as it would if he held the gun himself. I mean, he would've had to be double-jointed to position the gun on himself that way."

"Oh my God, slow down, slow down. I'm not sure this is all registering," Eileen said excitedly.

"I know, I know. I could hardly believe this myself. See, the gun was registered to *Mr.* Pagnotti, his father," Dr. Thomas continued.

"Oh my God!" Eileen exclaimed, her face lighting up and her jaw dropping as she realized at once what this meant.

"His father bought the gun just two weeks before the shooting. I mean, this is really crazy...it's not like his father really thought this through or anything...it's...it's like he almost didn't care, really. His son's fingerprints aren't even on the gun! And his son was shot from behind. And he was obviously hit hard from behind his head. He didn't get it falling because he was found lying face down. It's not like—"

"Oh my God! I cannot believe this," Eileen burst out.

"Wait! Wait! That's not all," Dr. Thomas said quickly. "As soon as Mr. Pagnotti starts getting questioned and confronted about all this, he just breaks down and starts telling the police he did this in self-defense! Self-defense! Can you believe this?"

"What self-defense? What? What else did they say? Was he being attacked?" Eileen asked looking more serious than dumbfounded now.

"No, no. I think he was saying he was being abused by his son, or something like that, like he couldn't take it anymore; that kind of thing," Dr. Thomas explained.

"Well, I don't doubt that for a minute. Brock was one sick man, let me tell you."

"And if you ask me—now this isn't something *they* said—but I'm sure his father must have thought that he could use you, you know, to blame this whole thing on. After he found that stuff on his son's computer, he probably thought he could just blame his son's suicide on this relationship—I'm not saying there was a relationship, you know—but the contact his son was having with you. You know what I mean? At least that's what he was arguing to

Mr. Strouse when he first contacted us after his son's death," said Dr. Thomas.

An awkward silence followed.

"Eileen...I know that—" Dr. Thomas started again, her voice now lowered and more composed, but Eileen cut her off, not wanting to hear what she had to say. She raised her hand to stop her and stood up to leave.

"No! Don't say anything, Diane. This is over," Eileen said.

"Over?" Dr. Thomas repeated with a puzzled look.

"Yes, it's over. I'm glad you're in better spirits now. I'm glad you don't have to worry about whether you're being sued or how this will all look to anybody—the insurance companies or news media or whoever—"

"Eileen!"

"No, just listen to me," Eileen insisted, shutting her eyes and shaking her head. "Just listen. I made a mistake; I'm not about to make another. I'm resigning, okay Diane? Effective right now."

"Eileen, please, you're talking nonsense," Dr. Thomas argued.

"Am I? Well then nonsense it will have to be, Diane. I'm sorry you hear it that way. But you know what the real nonsense is, Diane? The real nonsense was caring more about whether you're going to be sued or how this would all look, than about me or how I was doing or about what the truth was. You were concerned with the superficiality of it—the impression it gave. You were selfish, that's all you were."

"Eileen, I can't believe what you're saying. You know, I thought I would bring you in here to talk about what needed to happen to help save your job," said Dr. Thomas indignantly. "There's still the issue of you having contact with your patient...you know, online with the chatting and all that, Eileen. I'm shocked by your attitude. I really don't understand it."

"I don't expect you to. I really don't. But I'm not interested in staying here. I'm not even sure if I'm interested in staying in this field, to tell you the truth. I want to start over, and this is not a place where I can do that.

"I was stupid, and I used very bad judgment in what I did. I don't care whether or not you believe me now, but I didn't know it was my patient—"

"Eileen, I *do* believe you—"

"Yes, well, whatever, Diane. I'm sure you do. You sound very convinced," she replied sarcastically. "But I didn't know it was my patient. He wasn't who I thought he was, and I wasn't who he thought *I* was. And I know that goes on a lot in these online chats, but you know what? That goes on here too?"

"You're not making any sense, Eileen," Dr. Thomas said.

"It goes on here, it goes on everywhere. You always have to be on the lookout for people pretending to be something their not, for people giving you a false impression. I've been a victim of it my whole life, Diane...my whole life. I grew up having to pretend to be something I'm not or to pretend I wasn't upset or angry. I had to pretend everything was just wonderful. But it's stopping now. I want real people in my life. And for now it's going to start with my mother. That's all I care about right now—fixing things between me and my mother."

"Eileen, look, I understand where you're coming from. I don't agree with you, but I think you've been through a lot. Listen, I do want you to come back. I want you to at least take some time to think about this," Dr. Thomas insisted.

"I appreciate that, Diane. I really do. But I can't help feeling that maybe what you really need is just to get things all nice and tidy so you can put this behind you. I'm not so sure your concern is me."

Dr. Thomas's mouth was agape as she listened to Eileen continue.

"Look, I need to get on with my life, and it's not going to happen here. And besides, I'm not irreplaceable," Eileen said with a smirk. "You can replace me, I'm sure. But that's just the point. I need to be in some place in my life where the people are not parts that are so interchangeable. I want to care and feel cared about."

"Eileen!"

"No. It was a pleasure. I learned a lot. Thank you...really," said Eileen as she extended her hand to Dr. Thomas, who clumsily stuck her hand out by reflex. They shook hands, and Eileen walked out the door.

She drove home that afternoon for the last time from Milltown Community Mental Health Center. The roads were sprinkled with dirt and sand from the storm a few days earlier, so she drove slowly along her three-minute commute home. The sun shone brightly against a clear blue sky, thawing the ground where there remained just scattered patches of snow on the parts of lawns that were forever trapped in shadows. Her mind was clear, and her body was relaxed. She felt good.

Eileen arrived home, pleased to see her mother's car still parked in the driveway. She went inside, took her coat off and hung it up. She walked into the kitchen, where her mother—who had a pot of water on the stove—hugged her briefly. Eileen took out a couple of mugs and two tea bags while her mother poured the hot water. They sat down, sipped their tea, looked at each other and talked. No typing, no pointing, no clicking—just talking.

The End

About the Author

RICHARD CARR is a clinical psychologist with 35 years of experience in settings similar to those portrayed in e-Therapy. Readers will be drawn to his unique voice as an author, shaped by his intimate knowledge of the therapeutic process and the complexities of mental health. His expertise lends credibility to the story, offering readers a rare glimpse into the world of psychotherapy and the challenges faced by both patients and therapists.

Printed in the United States
by Baker & Taylor Publisher Services